Divining Bliss
The Sydney Roberts Series—Book Three

Susan Hart Snyder

www.susanhartsnyder.com

Cover design by Micah Kearns
Author photo by Patti Sewall

Divining Bliss/ Susan Hart Snyder -- 1st Ed.

ISBN 978-0-9974224-3-6

To Lincoln and James,
who taught me that to find your bliss,
you need look no further
than the back seat of the family car
as it moseys down a two-lane highway
on a starry starry night.

You don't reach Serendib by plotting a course for it.
You have to set out in good faith for elsewhere
and lose your bearings serendipitously.
—JOHN BARTH

Brr. Half-asleep and snuggling deeper into my lumpy motorhome mattress, I wondered why I was so cold. My RV was an old one, but when I went to bed the little heater was working fine.

Technically the RV wasn't mine. I inherited it from my Uncle George and traded it to my cousin, Ralph, for a few months' rent in his basement apartment in the Bronx. The only condition was I deliver it to him in New York. It was the means I used to say good-bye to a lifetime spent in Southern California and to start my life over in the East. I had only been there a few weeks, however, when I had to borrow the motorhome back in order to leave New York in a hurry. Traveling the country in a behemoth vehicle wasn't high on my bucket list, so it was my intention to return it to him somehow, at some point.

Tapping my hand around, I discovered my rotund black and white cat Alice curled up under the covers with me, and for once I welcomed her company. But even with her fury warmth there was no going back to sleep.

I clicked the switch on the bedside lamp. No light. Hmm.

As I threw my legs over the side of the bed, I strained my eyes through the early morning darkness to check for Mr. Bumbles, my Basset Hound. Due to the cold nights, he had been sleeping in the motorhome with me instead of outside in Calvin Wheatly's junkyard with his coonhounds. Generously speaking, our "campsite" was actually an automotive repair shop and Cal was a good, albeit agonizingly slow, mechanic. He and his coonhounds came into my life when during my journey to New York the motorhome coughed and died right outside of Harmony, a dusty little town in the red rocks area of Southern Utah.

I needed Cal then and I needed him now. My speedy exit from the Bronx was due to my knowing far too much for my health about the workings of a human-trafficking ring. Its leader, an Irish pub owner named Carrick, was a happy-go-lucky storyteller when he wasn't ordering executions. After being kidnapped by his gang for a nightmarish two days that left me with some nasty bumps and bruises, I was rescued by law enforcement officers assigned to break up the ring.

The lead agent was a man named Malachi Keane, who was also Irish. I was still a bit fuzzy as to exactly who he worked for–FBI? NYPD? He wasn't letting me in on it. The officers working for him did let me know, however, that if I wanted to make it to my next birthday I needed to find an off-the-grid place to park myself.

And so it was back to Harmony for me, the most off-the-grid place a body could ask for.

Sliding my foot along the floor until I came into contact with Mr. Bumbles' tail, I stood up. Ever the loyal hound, I knew he would be stretched out on his side not far from me, and in the darkness I didn't want to trip on him. I found one of my sweaters in the bedside drawer and slipped it on over my pajama top then my robe over it. I figured the extension cord Cal plugged into my motorhome had come loose and was the reason the electricity wasn't working.

When I stepped outside, flashlight in hand, Mr. Bumbles was right there behind me, tags jingling. Our inspection of the extension cord revealed it was plugged in tight, so I decided to follow it. Bending down and stroking the top of Mr. B's silky head, I hesitated before picking my way through Cal's stockpile of rust–a lovely way to start the day.

It was slow going as we followed the beam of my flashlight along the orange cord, making our way around car carcasses and stacks of used tires. To Cal's credit, we hadn't come across one pile of coonhound caca. Maybe the guy was more fastidious than I thought. Right.

With my eyes focused on the ground I didn't notice the second beam of light until it was right on top of us, but Mr. B had sniffed out his coonhound pals. He trotted over to them as they and Cal approached.

"Whatcha lookin' for?" he asked, shining his light right at me.

"The electricity's off in the motorhome." I blinked and turned away from him.

"The whole place is gone dark. Didn't ya notice?" He cast his flashlight beam from the yard to his shop then to his apartment up above it like a searchlight advertising a movie premiere.

"No, I hadn't noticed." It always seemed pretty dark in Cal's yard with his security lights covered in layers of dust and grease. "What do you think's the matter?"

"Probably just a breaker switch. I was just headin' round back to check the electrical panel." Pointing his flashlight out in front of him, he walked past me.

I followed him, wanting to see the source of power for the motorhome in case I needed to deal with it myself at some point. I wasn't anticipating being with Cal too long, but that's what I thought the last time, and it ended up being eight days. One of my goals for the day was to get a hold of Malachi and find out if there had been any progress on catching Carrick and his gang. The other agents made it sound like it could be a long haul. But long was relative. Did that mean a few days or a few weeks?

"Tarnation!" Cal yelled into the dark, stopping short, so I almost ran into him. Taking off his cap, he slapped it hard against his thigh.

"What's the matter?" I took a step back.

"Look at 'er!" He pointed his flashlight at a large metal box that was dangling by a few wires from the rear wall of his shop.

Recognizing the box as an electrical panel, but not at all comprehending how it could have gotten in that state, I asked, "Why is it hanging like that? Did it fall?"

"Of course not, woman!" Cal walked closer to it, but didn't touch it. "Some lousy thieves did this. Picked the thing clean of copper wire!"

Normally a pretty patient guy, Cal was the maddest I had ever seen him. In a role reversal, since he was usually the one dealing with *my* temper, I kept my voice calm and asked, "Why would they want your copper wire?"

"Money."

"Is it worth that much?"

"Metal theft is big business. Railroad signal lines, scrap metal, manhole covers, anywheres they can get their filthy hands on it."

"Manhole covers!" If I had wanted to make Cal even madder I would've laughed out loud on that one, visualizing a thief trying to hide a manhole cover under his trench coat.

"Thing is, though," he said, putting his cap back on his head and tugging hard at the brim until it was down to his brows, "they make maybe, what, sixty bucks off the copper they steal from this place? But it's gonna cost me a passel a dough to repair her."

"You can do it yourself?" I shined my own flashlight on the box. It looked pretty complicated.

"Most. But I ain't touchin' her 'til the utility company does their repair and gives me the okay."

"Dangerous?"

"Mighty. Fact is the only good news comin' out of the metal theft business is when every once in a while the authorities find some joker prone-dead at a sub-station fried to a crisp."

"I think they call that divine justice." I understood Cal's desire for retribution, but at the same time was disturbed by the vision of a smoldering corpse.

"You got that one right." He turned his back on the box. "I best let Deputy Crane know. This is likely only the beginning of a problem for Harmony."

"You think they'll do it again?"

"They'll work the area for sure, now that they got away with this one. Never would have either if the hounds had been in the yard. My dogs woulda chased 'em right off. Was just too cold last night to make 'em sleep outside."

"It's still cold." I tugged on my robe. "Sounds like it's going to be a while before we have any electricity."

"That's right. Could be a day or two, but I'll get her up as soon as I can. Meantime, you may want to find another place to roost."

"I'll think about it." I felt really uncomfortable about having to ask a favor of anyone else in town. I already owed Cal for letting me park my motorhome in his yard. Then there was V.A. Loomis, the local dentist who had taken care of a chipped tooth for me on my previous unscheduled stop in Harmony. She was my source for hot showers, an invaluable kindness. No, I had racked up enough debt for one little town. I didn't need to go asking around about a place to stay. I could survive the cold and lack of electricity for two nights. After all, I had Alice—she was a great hot water bottle and rarely left the bed.

"Hey, Cal," I called after him as he started toward his shop. I was thinking about the favors he had done for me.

"Yeah?" He turned his flashlight back on me.

I shielded my eyes with a cupped palm, thinking Cal enjoyed his flashlight a little too much. "Let me buy you breakfast at Dusty's." Dusty's was the favorite local diner, or make that the *only* diner or restaurant of any kind in town. Fortunately Dusty, the owner, was not only a good guy, but also a great cook. I had become addicted to his buffalo Bolognese during my previous time in Harmony.

"Huh?" Cal acted like he didn't understand the question.

"Breakfast."

"Yeah?"

"Without electricity, you're not going to be able to cook this morning. I'd like to treat you to breakfast at Dusty's."

After he deliberated so long I was about to repeat the question, he nodded his head. "All right. All right. That sounds okay." I guess offers like mine didn't come along too often for Cal.

"Good."

"Gotta meet with Crane first."

"That's fine. No hurry. I'll check on you in a while."

"Right." He turned around and continued on to his shop.

I spent the next hour in bed with every blanket and coat I owned piled on top of Alice and me. When the sun was bright enough to provide the light I needed, it was time to throw myself together. Pulling back the covers to make sure Alice hadn't been crushed by the weight, I stroked her under her chin. She stretched her body out to its full length then curled right back up. I pulled the covers over her, minus the jackets. "Have a nice day, you lazy cat."

Hearing voices coming from the shop, I zipped up my warmest jacket, pulled the hood over my head and made my way over there. If I was going to survive Southern Utah's high-desert winter I needed to load up on more cold-weather clothing. But was I even going to be in Utah for the winter? I had no idea.

When I walked into the shop, I found Mr. Bumbles and the coonhounds spread out in various stages of sniffing and scratching. Deputy Patrick Crane and Cal were over by the workbench, with the deputy bent over a notebook and Cal resting one hip against the bench while twirling a toothpick between his fingers. He had hung a large battery-operated light from a nail on a pegboard at the back of the bench. It was doing a good job of cutting through the dim interior.

"Hey there," I said as I approached them.

"Hi, Sydney." The deputy looked up from his notebook.

"Patrick," I responded. The two of us had moved to a first-name basis during my previous stay in Harmony in the course of several meetings regarding Floyd and Lloyd Bailey, twin teen mini-mobsters, who tagged my RV. "Are you two still in the middle of things?" I looked from one to the other.

"Just finishing up," Patrick said.

"Cal filled me in on the metal theft business earlier this morning. He seemed to think this was the first case for Harmony."

"True, we haven't had any trouble with it, at least not in the time I've been here, but it's a huge problem for every state in the union."

"It sure doesn't sound like a very lucrative crime with metal not being worth that much. Why would someone risk being electrocuted for sixty dollars?"

"The individuals stealing it are usually addicts, desperate for a fix. They don't make a lot and they often trip up." Patrick closed his notebook and straightened his tall thin frame to his full height. "The gangs, on the other hand, have it figured out. They recruit juvenile members by enticing them with a cut of the take, and then they send them out to do the stealing. Smart. No risk to the gang leaders of falling or being electrocuted."

"Nice guys."

"Oh, yeah, real gems." He turned to Cal. "I'll get on this, call over to St. George and a few other spots, see what kind of metal theft activity has been going on in the area."

"That's good by me." Cal leaned away from the bench. "I'd sure like to see the look on them no-good faces from the other side of prison bars the amount of trouble and dollars they gonna cost me."

"We'll see what we can do." Patrick took a step toward the entrance. "I'll keep in touch."

"Are you heading to Dusty's for breakfast?" I asked, knowing that Dusty's was part of Patrick's daily routine.

"Yeah, I am."

"We'll walk over with you. Or, did you bring your car?"

"Nah. I walked. Sun's out. It's a nice morning."

"Yeah, if you like to freeze." Sticking my hands in my pockets, I turned to Cal. "Are you about ready?"

"Just need to grab my coat."

"Great. We'll meet you at the gate." I turned and started for the yard with Patrick following behind me.

"What's the latest on the Bailey boys?" I asked as we stood waiting for Cal. "Were they ever disciplined for burglarizing Mrs. Anderson's house?"

"Yeah, they were."

"How about that. I thought for sure their mother would have figured out a way to keep her precious little brats from paying for their crimes."

"They were sentenced to sixty days on a juvenile work project." Patrick turned up the collar of his jacket.

"You mean they actually have to scrub public toilets with a toothbrush?"

"Something like that." He smiled.

"Good to know that justice was served." I smiled back.

CHAPTER TWO

When we walked into Dusty's, I suggested to Cal that we eat with Patrick at the counter. At a booth, with just each other for company, I was pretty sure Cal and I would run out of things to talk about right after the coffee was poured. That is, unless I was willing to engage in a detailed discussion about hunting.

The diner was full of locals. Who else would there be? Unfortunately, one of those included Genevieve Bailey, the Bailey boys' mother–speak of the devil–with a personality as brash as her blonde hair. She was not fond of Patrick, who dared go after her little criminals for their illegal activity. She didn't like me either, especially after I confronted her when she rudely interrupted our buffalo steak night dinner at Dusty's and we exchanged heated words. With my having been gone for a while and her self-absorption, I wondered if she would even remember me.

As we passed by Genevieve's table, she turned her eyes up at Patrick and glared at him. When they shifted to me, I watched her look turn from confusion to disdain. Yeah, she remembered me.

Making sure Cal ended up between Patrick and me in case the two of us *did* run out of things to say, I slid onto my stool. Dori Hunt, the waitress I became friends with on my previous stop in Harmony, was at the far end of the counter taking an order. Dori and her brother, Luke, had been born into a group of polygamists that threw them out because Dori had been too rebellious and Luke hadn't met their expectations for a son. Dori hadn't talked much about the differences in Luke that made them reject him, but I speculated from his behaviors that he was probably autistic.

Only in her mid-twenties, Dori was a feisty advocate for the oppressed. At the same time I left Harmony to continue on to New York, she and Luke moved to L.A., a long-time dream of hers. My ex, Harry, a big-hearted guy, helped her get a job at a restaurant in Hollywood owned by a friend of his and also helped her find an apartment. Harry even managed to develop a relationship with Luke.

And they would have still been there, if not for my snooping into Carrick's trafficking ring. On one of my calls to her from New York, Dori mentioned that the women's shelter where she had just started volunteering sometimes helped victims of trafficking. I asked her to find out if anyone there had heard of the Rock cartel. Egomaniac that he was, Carrick named his evil enterprise after himself–Carrick means rock in Gaelic. With tentacles that reached across the country and our borders, the cartel soon got wind of Dori's questions, which put her right in their path. She and Luke were forced to hide out in Harmony with me, but she had no intention of remaining any longer than two seconds after she received the all clear from Malachi.

Breakfast had been quite pleasant. I left most of the talking to Cal and Patrick, who had a lot more in common than I thought. Cal was surprisingly well versed in current events, considering he didn't have a TV and I was pretty sure he didn't receive home delivery of *The Wall Street Journal.* Turns out he's an avid listener of *NPR.* Who knew?

Catching Dori's eye, I signaled that I needed a refill on my coffee. I was just about to turn back to my plate when two very large breasts, which stretched the threads of a red-ribbed sweater to their breaking point, filled my vision. Oh, no. It was far too early in the day for a conversation with Genevieve. Actually, there was never a good time for a visit from her. But there she was, squeezing onto the stool next to mine.

"So, you're back." She turned so she was facing me and tossed one side of her lifeless blonde hair over her shoulder.

"That's right."

"What was your name again, honey?"

Honey? Oh, boy, that nickname sat with me just about as well as *Missy.* "Sydney." I grabbed my purse from the back of my stool so she'd think I was leaving.

"Couldn't keep away from Noah, huh?" She leaned her right elbow on the counter and rested her cheek on her fist.

"What!" I spat out before I could stop myself. Where did that come from?

"It was obvious you had the hots for him last time you were here. Why else would you come back to this hellhole?"

Nice. Calling her own town a hellhole. When I turned from her to see if Cal and Patrick had heard any of the conversation, I was met with two pairs of eyes staring right back at me. From the other side of the counter, Dori joined the group, coffee pot in hand. Oh, yeah, I had an audience.

"You shouldn't have wasted your gas, honey. Noah is not a one-woman man. He's had lots of women and threw them all back."

"It's *Sydney*," was all I managed to get out, dumbstruck by her vulgarity and working hard to hold off my rising anger. I didn't want to stoop to her level.

"Well, Sydney, if you want my advice," Genevieve leaned so far into the counter she was using it as a shelf for her balloon boobs, "I'd turn that red head of yours right around and scoot on out of here. Find a place where there are so many men you're sure to nab one who goes for Amazon types like you."

I looked up at Dori in disbelief. Before I could come up with a good reply, which for me generally takes until the next day, Dori said, "And you, Genevieve, ought to pack up those quadruple-D implants of yours, along with that fried and dyed hair, and head for Dollywood, where you'd fit right in!"

"Jealous?" Genevieve straightened in her chair and shook her shoulders, her breasts jiggling. "Perhaps if you ever decided to stop dressing like some braless California hippie, one of those polygamist uncles of yours would be willing to take you back and make you his seventeenth wife."

Growing very quiet and narrowing her eyes, Dori held the coffee pot out and tipped it toward Genevieve's arm. "Coffee?" Her voice was low and threatening.

"No! Get that away from me!" Genevieve jerked back.

"Dori, can I get some coffee down here?" Patrick's voice cut through the tension. "Dori," he said again when she didn't respond right away.

Finally turning away from Genevieve, she walked over to Patrick and filled his cup.

"If you'd burned me, I would've sued you," Genevieve said loudly.

Ignoring her as if she hadn't heard, Dori said to Cal in her friendliest waitress voice, "Would you like me to top that off for you?"

"Why sure," Cal said, also in a tone that suggested nothing had happened.

When she realized she was no longer going to get Dori's attention, Genevieve stood up, set her hand on my shoulder, and leaned into my ear. "If you don't want to get hurt, honey, you think about what I said. Do all the sexual favors you want for Noah, but there's no way you're ever going to keep him interested."

Brushing her hand off my shoulder like it was an errant piece of lint and biting my tongue, I turned my back on her and toward Cal. That woman was *not* going to bait me. When he saw my distress, Cal said, "Sydney, what was you sayin' about New York City?"

I took a breath and shook off my desire to pull Genevieve's blonde hair out by its dark roots. "I believe I was telling you about how dogs can be off leash in Manhattan parks early in the morning and they don't seem to bother each other."

"That could be," Cal picked right up on the topic. "Off leash, dogs aren't as territorial. There's no good reason for 'em to fight." Either ignoring or forgetting the exchange with Genevieve, Cal started in on an explanation of canine behavior. Thank God for Cal. In his own unique way, he knew how to save the day.

Hearing Genevieve's loud footsteps tapping against the floor, I started to relax my shoulders, however she hadn't quite run out of ammunition. Stopping a few feet behind us, she hissed, "Don't think I've forgotten what you did to my boys, Crane. As miserable as things are going to get for you in this town, you may want to think about taking the same train out with your lady friends."

"Good-bye, Genevieve." Patrick lifted his hand and waved at her without turning around.

"That woman," Dori said when the echoing of Genevieve's heels finally followed her out the door.

When Cal finally finished his discourse on dogs and as Dori was writing up my tab, she asked if I wanted to go with her to see Ruthie, a child bride of Samuel Vaullie's. He was the abusive leader of a local polygamist cult and had endangered Ruthie's life when he neglected to get her proper help during the delivery of her baby. Two other young women from his cult had died in childbirth. He covered their deaths by secretly burying them and their babies in the yard of the town doctor and drunk.

Doctor Norman Schrum was the attending physician at all three of those births, and Ruthie was the only one to come out alive–no thanks to him–or Samuel. Those two were in an unholy alliance, sealed by the devil. Schrum was in line to pay for his sins, tucked away in jail, awaiting trial. Samuel, however, was on the run. I had spotted him a few days before in the back of a sedan at a gas station just outside of St. George. I alerted Patrick, who had put the word out to other law enforcement agencies to be on the lookout for him. So far, there were no other leads.

Ruthie was being cared for by V.A. Loomis' mothers at the family ranch–*mothers*, as in, she had two of them. Some members of her family were practicing polygamists, but it was explained to me that in their particular group they had the freedom to choose whether or not to partake in the multiple wives thing. Based on my growing knowledge of polygamists, I doubted that any woman or child in those cults had the right to *choose* anything.

Running through our schedules–like I had anything on mine other than my editing work–Dori and I decided we would try to see Ruthie that afternoon. I had retained my copy editor position at the Manhattan publishing house that hired me after my move to New York. My boss offered to let me telecommute when I told her I needed an extended leave due to a "family emergency." It was a lie, but I wasn't sure how she would react to the whole human-trafficking gang story. And I needed the job. It was important to keep Alice and Mr. Bumbles in the manner to which they'd become accustomed– that is, in canned chicken livers, kibble and, of course, Fritos. I told Dori I would call V.A. to find out if it would be all right with her mothers if we came for a visit, and I would get back to her about the particulars.

As I was putting my wallet back in my purse, it dawned on me that I wasn't going to be able to do any editing until Cal got the electricity going again. Seeing Dusty's torso through the pass-through to the kitchen, I decided to ask if he'd mind if I brought my work to the diner.

He was delighted at the prospect of turning his place into an Internet cafe. It could start a trend. Sure.

CHAPTER THREE

As Cal and I walked into his yard, I was concentrating so hard on my mental list of things I would need to take back to Dusty's later that morning that I somehow missed the giant horse standing in the middle of it. Atop the muscled beast was a stout middle-aged woman with a lined and tanned face and thin straight hair the same color as the horse's thundercloud-gray coat.

The sight was so shocking I just stood and stared. She stared right back–with disapproval in her eyes. As she looked from me to Cal and back again, I felt like I had been doused with a bucket of ice water–not a great feeling when I still hadn't warmed up from my cold start to the day.

"Hi, Honeybunch," I heard Cal say from where he was standing beside me.

Huh? I looked over at Cal. Did he call her *Honeybunch*?

Her response was to methodically dismount from the horse, lead it over to Cal's tow truck and tie the reins to the door handle. Then she walked over to us and stood with her weight evenly distributed over her thick thighs, her sizable fists dug into her waist. "So, this is how you've been spending your time." She bore her small light brown eyes into him and jutted her chin at me.

"Whatcha mean there, Honeybunch?"

Sneaking a peak at him and noticing he looked pretty calm for someone who was about to meet a firing squad, I wondered if he really didn't get it.

"Took a liking to redheads, huh?" She narrowed her focus to my head.

Really? Did it have to be about the hair? Always?

"What, *her*?" Comprehension finally dawned on Cal as he sized me up like I was roadkill.

"Yeah, her." She joined in the roadkill assessment.

Was there a *kick me* sign on my jacket when I left the motorhome that morning? First Genevieve, now Honeybunch? That woman sure didn't look like any Honeybunch to me as she clenched and unclenched her jaw.

"I wondered why it had been so long since you had me over," she hissed, cemented to her spot on Cal's dirt-covered yard.

Did Cal entertain women in his apartment over the shop? Casting my eyes upward, I imagined a studio-size place decorated in camouflage and dirty rags, with stuffed boar, bear and deer staring down from their final resting places on his walls.

"But, you ain't been around, Honeybunch. You been out east at your sister's, right?"

"Last month." She narrowed her eyes to slits. "You know I've been back for a while. Least you could've done was to tell me you had another woman." She ran her piercing glare all the way from my head to my feet.

"I don't have any interest in *her*." His look said I had deteriorated from roadkill to the crap clinging to the sole of boots that had tramped through a pigsty. "I'm just helpin' her out."

"I bet you are–a woman like that." She wrinkled her nose at me in disgust.

Okay. That was it! "You have totally misread the situation." I held my hand out to the motorhome. "Cal helped me out with my RV when it broke down here a couple months ago, and is letting me park it here again for a few days until I can move on."

"Oh, so you're staying here too? Isn't that convenient."

"No! Yes," I sputtered. "But, that's it. I have absolutely zero romantic interest in Cal."

"So, you're saying he's not good enough for you?"

"No, that's not what I'm saying." I shook my head. I was getting confused. "Cal's a great guy."

"Yeah? And, last time I checked he was mine! Is that still the case, Cal? Or, has she lured you into her trap, as I suspect?"

Cal, who had taken a step away from me, seemed to be content with fading into the background. Caught in her crosshairs, however, he decided to speak up. "I'm not interested in her. She's got a terrible temper."

"I do not!"

"Do too." He looked at me like I was an untrainable coonhound. "You gotta admit you're short on patience."

"Thanks!"

"You do have some fair qualities, too." He put his hand on his chin and stared at me like he was trying to come up with some.

"Good of you to say."

"See there," the woman interjected, "you wouldn't be carrying on like that if there wasn't something between you two."

"No!" I said, loudly, "No! No! No! There's *nothing* between us!"

"Is that right, Cal?" She took a step toward him, her eyes locked on his. "There's no funny stuff going on?"

"No, Honeybunch. You're the only woman in my life. There's no need for anyone else."

Taking a long deep breath, contemplating Cal's version of a true love vow, she finally released her fists from her waist, took a step toward him and patted his shoulder like she was reassuring her horse. "All right, then. Let's just keep it that way."

Suddenly aware of a presence behind me, I turned around to see Noah Thompson standing there. Great! How long had *he* been there, and why hadn't he come to my defense? Noah, a local rancher, and I had a short and pleasurable fling during my first unscheduled visit to Harmony, which resumed two days into this second stopover. I had no intention of ever seeing him again when I left for New York, but I was finding his classic cowboy looks and calm strength of character impossible to resist.

With the attention drawn to him, he stepped into our happy little circle. "Lou," he said, removing his hat and nodding at her. "Cal." He nodded at him also.

"Noah, good to see you!" The woman's demeanor did a one-eighty. "How are your mama and daddy?"

"Just fine. Thanks for asking. And yours? How are they?"

"Never change." She combed her fingers through her hair and pulled it into a ponytail she held with one hand. "Daddy's still up on his horse every morning, making the rounds, and mama's still managing the place." She smiled brightly, letting her hair fall back to her shoulders. "It's darn good to see you."

She reached out and patted Noah's shoulder, just as she had Cal's.

Was that her entire repertoire of public displays of affection? And, was she flirting with Noah? After giving *me* such a bad time? I flashed a questioning look at him.

"Lou, have you met Sydney?" Noah asked.

"Not in a manner of speaking. You know her?" She was back to her suspicious tone.

"I do. We're old friends." He looked over at me, turning up the corner of his mouth in a half grin. He was having way too much fun with the situation.

"You *are*?" Lou cocked her head.

"Sure. Lou, this is Sydney Roberts. Sydney, this is Lou Bryson."

"Nice to meet you." I reached out my hand.

Hesitating, she finally clasped my palm. "Hello." She studied my face like she was comparing it with one she had seen on a *Wanted* poster hanging in the post office.

Completely over being scrutinized by the woman, I dropped her hand. "I need to go. I've got work to get done today."

"Come on into the shop out of the wind," Lou said to Noah, speaking as if she had territorial rights to Cal's place. "We can talk there." Shifting so she blocked me from the group with her back, she was obviously delighted I was leaving.

"Thanks, but I can't stay for a visit." Noah reached out and put his hand on my arm before I had a chance to get away. "There are some things I need to discuss with Sydney."

"Oh?" Lou said, looking down where he was touching me.

"It was great to see you." Noah didn't elaborate.

Stepping out of his reach, I turned and started walking toward the motorhome and out from under Lou's cloud of condemnation. I had been belittled enough for one morning.

"Don't be a stranger," Lou said, as I felt Noah step in behind me. Then she changed her voice to a whisper loud enough to be heard at Dusty's. "My apologies, Cal, for believing it was you she was after. I thought Noah was too smart to be taken in by a woman like that. But then, men are weak."

"Oh, my God!" I said through clenched teeth, picking up the pace.

Putting his hand on the small of my back, Noah guided me toward the RV, then reached up and opened the door when we got to the steps.

"Who *is that* woman? And, doesn't she own a car?" I threw open my tiny refrigerator, yanking food out and setting it on the dinette, still seething from the encounter.

"She's one of the ranchers from a few miles west of town. Her family's been in the area a long time. She can come off a bit blunt."

"Ya think?" I leaned down and grabbed items from the bottom shelf.

"She means no harm."

"Sure." I looked up at him. "She'd run me down with that massive horse of hers the minute I turned my back."

"I doubt that."

"I don't!" I handed him a carton of yogurt.

"What are you doing?" Noah set the yogurt on the table.

"The electricity's out. Cal had his copper wire swiped sometime last night."

Noah whistled between his teeth. "That's not good."

"No, it's not. Cal's not happy about the money it's going to cost him, or the inconvenience."

"Does he have any idea who did it?"

"No. Patrick was over early this morning and will be trying to track down some leads. He said the thieves are likely to strike again in the area, so you probably should keep a lookout for them on your ranch."

"I will, and I'll let other folks know too." He looked down at the pile of food on the table. "What are you going to do with all of it?"

"Dusty said I could use the diner for my work. I'm going to ask him to store this food for me until the electricity is back on."

"I can take it to my place." Noah grabbed a jar of marmalade from me, set it down and leaned against the table. "And you along with it." Reaching his arms out, he pulled me into him until our faces were a breath away from each other. "Doesn't that sound a whole lot better than the diner? Nice and quiet. Plenty of room to spread out." He kissed the tip of my nose.

"No, I'm good. I've got it worked out."

"Great company." He kissed my neck just above the collar of my jacket.

"That's what I'm afraid of." I willed myself not to give in.

He raised his head so that we were eye to eye once again. "This motorhome is really cold. Do you plan on bunking with Dusty too?"

"Of course not! I'll use his place during the day and come back in the evenings."

"And what? Sit around in the cold and dark?"

"I'll buy candles."

"Oh, that'll help. And how are you going to keep warm?"

"I have Alice."

"Your cat? When you could have me?" His eyes danced as he leaned in, pressed his body into mine and kissed me tenderly at first then with a depth that made me see stars.

I came up for air, barely hanging on to my last thread of resistance. "If the repair seems like it's going to take a long time I'll move this thing to V.A.'s. She offered when I first got back."

"And I'm offering now. Make that, I'm insisting." He locked his eyes on mine. "We can move it to my place this morning."

I expelled my breath. Oh boy, what to do? Our relationship was a strange one. It was intense, but I had no idea where it was going, especially since I didn't even know where *I* was going once Malachi had arrested the gang members. "There's Mr. Bumbles to consider." It was amazing how useful Mr. B could be when I needed to defer a decision.

"You know he'll love my place. Consider him considered."

"Okay, then." I relented, realizing it really would be much easier to move the motorhome to where I would have electricity than move half my life to Dusty's. "But I'm staying in the motorhome on your property, not at your house. Will you be able to hook me up?" Shoot! Did I just say that? My face flushed as soon as the words left my mouth.

Noah turned up the corner of his. "Oh yeah, I think I can manage to hook you up." Then he bent in and kissed me again.

"All right." I pulled away from him, turned around and opened the refrigerator door once again. "Hand me the food. I'll get it back in here."

When everything was put away, I stood up. "I'll call Dusty and let him know to shelve his plans for becoming Harmony's newest and only Internet cafe."

"I don't expect techies were going to be flooding the place with business anyway."

"No. I expect not." I hugged my arms to my chest. "Do you mind if I move this thing to your place right away. The sun doesn't seem to be doing a very good job of warming it up."

"That's fine. Just give me a head start and I'll clear a place that'll be easy for you to pull into." He set his hat on his head.

"Thanks. I'll let Cal know I'm leaving, but maybe I'll call instead of going over there. Wouldn't want to give Lou any more ammunition."

"You and Cal." He grinned. "Now there's a picture."

"Not one for my album." I grinned back.

As Noah put his hand on the doorknob to leave, I asked, "What was it that you came here to discuss?"

"This." He let go of the doorknob, closed the gap between us and hugged me to his chest. No kissing. Just a comfy bear hug. Releasing me, he said, "And I wanted to invite you to the annual round dance. It's this Saturday night in my barn."

"*Round* dance? Don't you mean *square* dance?"

"No. It's round dance."

"Never heard of it."

"They're real popular."

"In one tiny corner of the world called Harmony, Utah?" I said.

"No. All over. Look it up. You'll be surprised."

"No. I probably won't. I'm beginning to think there's nothing in Harmony that would surprise me."

"So, you're coming."

"Sure. If it's as popular as you say, I've gotta see what I've been missing."

CHAPTER FOUR

After I moved the motorhome onto Noah's ranch, and he took off to fence the back forty or whatever cowboys do, V.A. and Dori swung by to take me to V.A.'s family ranch. It was the next one over from Noah's. So, there we were, riding along in the cab of V.A.'s truck, V.A., Dori, and I, like the oddest mishmash of girlfriends ever. V.A. was entertaining us with the story of a cattle drive she participated in, moving a herd down to the valley from a mountain pasture. She was almost giddy–a word not often associated with V.A.–when she got to the part about the greenhorn who had signed on for the adventure, but couldn't manage to keep his horse from running away with him.

I was waiting for her to bring up my own *greenhorn* experience with her, not a fond memory. On my previous stop in Harmony, she had enlisted me to help with a calving. The cow and calf had done fine. I, on the other hand, was really no help at all. I ended up covered in cow poop and with a bruised tailbone.

Fortunately, Dori interjected her own animal husbandry story before V.A. had a chance to reminisce about my inadequacies as a ranch hand.

Looking over at the two women from my spot by the passenger door, I thought they couldn't have been more different from the women I had socialized with in New York. My cousin Ralph's girlfriend and her friends were nice enough, but it was tough to find a real person to connect with under all the makeup, spandex and attitude.

With V.A. and Dori, however, you knew exactly who they were and where you stood with them. They were as clear as the blue sky that arched over Harmony. V.A. was six feet of no nonsense, served up with simple kindness, and sublimely content with her life in Southern Utah. Dori was a smaller but also mighty force, for social justice in particular. She had worlds to conquer and wasn't going to let anything stand in the way of that. Although they were over a decade apart in age, as descendants of pioneers whose beliefs drove them into vast, arid, and empty spaces, they shared virtual, if not literal, DNA. And, it shaped them in ways that made me want to be around them–something I was just beginning to appreciate.

When I called that morning to ask V.A. about the possibility of Dori and I visiting Ruthie at the Loomis ranch she insisted on driving us. It was just as well, as I had yet to get around to asking Cal about the use of the hatchback I borrowed from him when I first got back to Harmony. I used it to bring Dori and Luke back from Los Angeles, and although I had a hard time fitting my tall frame into it I was considering renting it from him for the rest of my time in Harmony. As old as it was I figured he wouldn't charge me much, and *not much* was all I could afford.

Navigating over cattle guards and through the gates, V.A. pulled up in front of the ranch house. Her mother, Miriam, was just coming out of the barn. Tall like her daughter, she embraced V.A. after she stepped down from the cab and came around to the front of the truck to exchange hugs then escort us to the house.

We entered the living room by way of the kitchen. Odelia, V.A.'s father's second wife and the woman V.A. considered as much a mother to her as Miriam, was sitting in the same chair as when I last saw her. Older than Miriam, she used a walker to get around, which was next to her. "There you are, dear girl," Odelia said, as V.A. crossed the room to greet her.

"How's life treating you?" V.A. bent down to give her a peck on the cheek.

"I'm good enough to sit up and sip soup."

"Good to hear." V.A. straightened and turned toward us. "Ma, you know Dori."

"Of course."

"And you remember Sydney." V.A. nodded her head at me. "She was with me when I had to pull that calf a few months ago, and then we shared buffalo steak night with her."

Using both hands to slide her glasses back over her ears, she studied me for a moment and turned her voice up a couple of clicks. "Why, yes! I do recall your visit. How is that tailbone of yours?" She was hard of hearing, and seemed to adjust her volume according to the level of embarrassment contained in her statements.

"All better."

"That's good." Odelia nodded her head. "My husband Solomon had troubles with his tailbone. You remember that?" She looked over at Miriam, who had walked into the room carrying a tray with a teapot and mugs on it. "Sat on a donut for months."

"I believe Sydney's already heard that story." Miriam set the tray down on a side table next to the couch. "Herb tea, anyone?" She picked up the pot. "It's chamomile."

"I'd love some," Odelia spoke up before the rest of us had a chance to respond. "With a little milk, please."

Allowing a flicker of annoyance to cross her eyes before she responded, Miriam said, "I'll get to you in a minute, Odelia. Let me see what our guests want first. Sydney, how about you? Would you like some?"

"Sugar too," Odelia interjected before I had a chance to respond.

"Odelia, I'm going to serve them, and then I will get to yours," Miriam repeated louder and more slowly.

"I heard you. Put my hearing aids in this morning." Odelia reached around and adjusted the pillow at her back.

Head down so that we couldn't see her expression, Miriam expelled her breath and then picked up a cup. "Sydney?"

"Sure, but no milk or sugar, thanks."

"You don't know what you're missing," Odelia said in a singsong voice. "Nothing like a little sugar for an afternoon pick-me-up."

"She wants it plain," Miriam said flatly as she bent down to pour my tea.

Trouble in polygamy paradise? I sure wouldn't want to be stuck caring for my husband's second wife after he cut out for the Promised Land. Ma Odelia was now sitting straight up in her chair, watching every move Miriam made.

"Here, let me help you with that," V.A. walked over to Miriam. She was probably well practiced at running interference between the two of them. "You want some too, Dori?" She took the cup from her mother and walked it over to me.

"No, I'm good." Dori moved over to the couch, sat down, and crossed her legs.

"You sit down too," Miriam said to me. "V.A., why don't you go knock quietly on Ruthie's door and see if she'd like to join us. She must have gone to check on the baby."

After Miriam finally served Odelia her tea and Dori and I answered a barrage of questions about our whereabouts over the last few weeks, V.A. finally emerged from the hall. Thank goodness. There's only so many times you can explain that, yes, they do have trees in New York City and, no, the crowds don't bother me. Dori had to answer roughly the same questions about Los Angeles.

By mutual unspoken agreement, Dori and I managed to avoid any references to our being in Harmony to hide out from a cartel. The less people who knew the better. The cruelty toward human-trafficking victims I encountered in the Bronx was not too far removed from the way Samuel Vaullie treated his polygamist cult members. Miriam and Odelia had a history with Samuel's group, but V.A. claimed they didn't condone his behavior. That I believed, but what I still couldn't fathom was that they were okay with sharing a husband. How did the whole thing work? You get conjugal visits three days a week. I get three days a week. And on Sundays everybody rests?

V.A. walked into the room with a blanket-wrapped bundle lost in her arms, her nose six inches from the tiny face staring out from the swaddle. "Who's a sweet baby girl?" she said in a high-pitched voice. "Can you give me a little smile? Yes, you can. Yes, you can. Smile now at your Auntie V.A. Come on now. Oh, you want to talk a little instead?" She tore her eyes away from the baby to speak to us. "Can you hear that?

She's cooing like a morning dove. So smart. She doesn't miss a thing."

Okay. About the last thing I ever expected to hear out of V.A.'s mouth was baby talk. It did fit with the way she patted your check when she was working on your teeth, however.

Ruthie appeared from behind V.A., dressed in a dull-colored long-sleeved blouse buttoned all the way to the top. At least she'd lost the Prairie Home Companion garb she wore the first time I saw her–a start if she was ever going to look her age, of which I had never been informed. In my head, I had her at fifteen. I made a mental note to ask Dori.

"Ruthie. Hi." Dori got up from the couch and approached her. "How *are* you?"

"Fine." She cast her eyes down in discomfort when she saw she was the center of attention.

"Come sit." Dori took her hand and led her to the couch.

"Do you want some tea, dear?" Miriam asked her.

"No, thank you. I just had a big glass of water."

"Good. Gotta keep hydrated when you're breastfeeding," V.A. said.

Reddening, Ruthie nodded her head.

"How's the whole mother thing going for you?" Dori asked, keeping hold of her hand.

"Good. Mama Miriam took Remy Elizabeth and me into St. George last week for her checkup, and the doctor said she's perfect." She smiled at her daughter.

"Remy Elizabeth. That's a great name!" I spoke up. That was another thing I had forgotten to ask. "How'd you come up with it?"

"I heard it."

"But, where?" I pressed, wondering how Ruthie could have heard anything with the way she had been kept so isolated.

"One time when Samuel took me with him to a store in St. George I heard a mother call it out to her daughter. I thought it was really pretty."

"It is. Is it from the Bible?"

"No. Remy means *from Reims*, a place in France where they crowned the kings. V.A. looked it up for me. But there was a Saint Reims." Ruthie looked over at Odelia and quickly glanced away. The old woman had probably given her a bad time for straying from the traditional. "And Elizabeth means *God's Promise*. She was the mother of John the Baptist."

"Well, it's beautiful," I said. "I'll bet Reims is beautiful too. And I hope the two of you get to visit it someday."

"Oh." Ruthie looked over at Remy with dawning realization in her eyes. The idea of the freedom she had gained by leaving Samuel's compound was so new to her she had barely begun to grasp it. Although it was wonderful that Miriam and Odelia took her in, Ruthie wasn't getting a lot of exposure to the outside world. The two women probably never strayed far from home.

"So, things have been going well for the two of you?" Dori asked.

"Yes." Ruthie pulled her long brown braid over her shoulder and started playing with the ends. "V.A. helped me sign up for online courses. When I finish them I'll be able to graduate from high school."

"That's wonderful!" Dori said.

"Great idea, V.A.!" I chimed in.

"Yep. And then she's going on to college, right Ruthie?" V.A. started pacing the room when Remy began to fuss.

"I hope so," Ruthie said, following Remy with her eyes. "Do you want me to take her?"

"May I?" Dori stood up. "I haven't gotten a close look yet."

V.A. walked over and gingerly passed Remy to Dori.

"She's so cute!" Dori said to Ruthie. "She's got your eyes."

"Thank you." Ruthie smiled up at her.

When Remy started to fuss again, Dori began circling the room, gently bobbing her up and down and making rhythmic shushing noises right in her face.

"What are you doing?" I asked. I had never seen anyone shush a baby like that, and it seemed to be working. Remy had immediately stopped fussing.

"Just calming her down."

"So, you're a baby whisperer too?"

"No. It's something I picked up at the women's shelter. There are usually a few infants around, and this is how the women are taught to soothe them."

"Maybe I should try it on my animals when they start to get skittery." Miriam laughed.

"Heck, I might even be able to use it on my patients when they come in hollerin' from a toothache." V.A. laughed too.

"Let me know if it works." Dori shifted her weight from side to side in an exaggerated rocking motion. "I may pick up a side business."

"Have you had any visitors?" I asked Ruthie, curious if anyone from Samuel's compound had come by.

"Noah's been over a few times, and Cal stopped by."

"Cal?" I asked in disbelief. Noah, I could almost understand, he lived so close by, but Cal?

"Yeah. He brought Remy a stuffed bunny."

"Really?" I hoped by stuffed she didn't mean one that he had personally shot and stuffed.

"Yeah. He's nice."

"Yes. He is," I said, thinking I couldn't recall Cal ever even mentioning Ruthie. I guess Harmony was just that small, or Cal really was that good a guy. "What about Mother Helen and other people from your group? Have they been by?"

"No." Ruthie looked down at her hands.

"We haven't seen a one of them," Odelia said in a loud, accusing tone. It was the first she had contributed to the conversation and, of course, it was a zinger. As quiet as she had gotten, I thought maybe she had turned her hearing aid down. Not a chance.

Miriam tried to catch Ma Odelia's eye before she continued. No luck.

"Those women should be ashamed of themselves!" Odelia stormed on. "That sinful, sinful man leaves Ruthie alone with a baby, and they're no help at all!"

Ruthie still hadn't raised her head, but we could tell she was sniffling. Getting up from her chair and walking over to Odelia, Miriam bent down and whispered something we couldn't hear. When she finished, she joined Ruthie on the couch and put her arm around her. Odelia sat with her prune mouth clamped shut, watching the two women. If she felt bad about making Ruthie cry, she sure didn't show it. I was really sorry I had broached the subject.

"It's okay, sweetheart." Miriam patted Ruthie's hand.

"I really miss them." Ruthie looked up, her eyes filled with tears.

"I know."

"And I'm worried about Angela. I had a nightmare about her–twice."

Angela was a young girl of about six who was likely to be Ruthie's half-sister, cousin, niece–no telling, really, with the way polygamist families intermarried. I had witnessed the harsh discipline leveled at her by Samuel Vaullie and his other wives, and thought that Ruthie's worry was warranted.

Dori stopped rocking, and said, "We can take you out there to see her."

"Really?" Ruthie asked.

"Sure." Dori looked over at V.A., who gave her a nod.

Odelia and Miriam were both frowning, either still peeved at each other or not keen on the idea of Ruthie going to the compound.

"How will they know we're coming?" Ruthie asked, referring to the fact that getting through to Samuel's cult was like trying to reach a live person at customer support.

"We'll just pop in," V.A. said, like she was going to visit a friendly next-door neighbor. "Tomorrow morning work for you?"

Nodding her head, her eyes still glassy, Ruthie said, "Yes. Thank you."

We stayed thirty more minutes, keeping the conversation light, then V.A. said she had to get back for a late afternoon patient.

"Would you like to hold her before you leave?" Ruthie asked me, looking down at Remy, who was quiet in her arms.

I hadn't had a turn holding the baby and sweet Ruthie apparently didn't want me to feel left out.

After hesitating a second, I said, "Well, sure." I had little experience with babies, and I was nervous about doing something wrong. When we both stood up and Ruthie handed Remy to me, however, the soft weight of her in my arms felt natural and timeless, like one of those experiences that are built into your genes. Looking down into her eyes, I was surprised at how clear they were and how penetrating her stare. "She's really checking me out. Isn't she kinda young to appear so wise?" I smiled.

"She's really smart." Ruthie beamed.

When I looked back down at Remy, she locked onto my eyes. Lost in them, I felt an otherworldly connection to her. How was that possible? Bending close enough to feel her soft breath on my skin, I whispered, "What are you trying to tell me, little one?" I came back to the present when Ruthie's shoulder brushed my arm and I looked over to find her staring. "I'm sure she's *very* smart," I said quickly. Before I returned Remy to her mother, however, I took one more whiff of eau de baby, a scent that should be bottled. That part I remembered from the few other times I held one.

When we turned onto the highway I told V.A. to take me to Cal's instead of back to the motorhome on Noah's ranch. Now that I was no longer walking distance from town, it was even more important I talk to him about renting the hatchback. Taking my phone out of my back pocket, I checked the time. Surely Lou would be long gone by then.

When we pulled up in front of Cal's, I asked Dori and V.A. if they were going to the round dance on Saturday night.

To my surprise, they both told me they never missed one. They also mentioned that there was going to be a practice the next afternoon at Dusty's for everyone who wanted to brush up on the steps. As I really didn't want to embarrass myself on the dance floor, I told them I'd be there, but I had little faith I was going to master the fine art of round dancing in one session.

Cal was by himself when I found him outside in his yard, his head under the hood of an old truck. I took loud steps and cleared my throat as I approached. I had startled him once before while he was under the hood of another old vehicle, resulting in a nasty bruise on his head. I was not going to let it happen again.

"Hey, Cal." I joined him at the front of the truck and stared down at I-know-not-what. My dad taught me how to change a tire and add oil, but the lessons did not extend to engines. "Any luck with the electricity?"

"Got a hold of the electric company." He straightened up. "But they can't get out here 'til tomorrow, so it's gonna be a while yet before we can get the power back on."

"Sorry to hear that. Any word from Patrick?"

"Nah. Still early on." He shrugged.

"It was nice meeting your friend, Lou," I lied, telling myself I was just being polite, when I knew the real reason I brought her up was my inability to control my nosiness.

"She's a gem, that one." He pulled a toothpick out of his shirt pocket and held it between greasy fingers. "She can cut cattle faster 'n any man I ever seen."

"She cuts cattle? Why would she do that?" I pictured Lou atop her giant gray horse brandishing a twelve-inch knife. It fit. The poor cattle.

"'Cause it needs doin' if you got cattle." Cal scowled at me like I was a dimwit. "Competes in rodeos too. She's got a room full a ribbons."

"What *is* cutting exactly?" I was still not following.

"It's when you cut a group of cattle away from the herd–a single calf if it's for rodeo purposes."

"So, she doesn't actually cut them?"

"Nah." He shook his head.

"Good to hear." That was a relief.

"Unless she's castrating the bullocks."

"Oh." I pictured Lou wrestling a young bull–and winning. "You two been dating long?" I lead the conversation away from the nuances of raising cattle.

He looked down, trying to find the answer in his canvas boots. "Ten years, maybe."

"Wow! And this morning's the first I've ever seen her?"

"You ain't exactly a regular in these parts." His voice took on an edge that said he was losing patience with the probing.

"True." I was surprised at myself for feeling stung by the accusation.

"You could be, ya know." He softened his tone.

"I could be what?"

"A regular. You was crazy to leave this place for Boston."

"New York."

"Crazy all the same. And I was darn right. You're back before a third full moon."

The part of me that believed the only reason I came back to Harmony was because I was hiding out from the trafficking ring wanted to tell Cal exactly that. I thought it best, though, to let him think he was right, and for me to keep any other motive for my return to myself. "I want to talk to you about the hatchback." I dropped the subject. "I need a car while I'm here and was wondering if you'd rent it to me."

He sucked in his breath between his teeth. "I don't know about that. It was one thing to let you use her for a day, but she's my loaner for my customers while I'm fixin' their vehicles. Not sure I'd want to have her tied up."

Judging from the layer of dust and cobwebs on that car when I borrowed it, my drive to L.A. was the first time it had moved from the corner of his yard in years. Moving past my incredulity, I said, "How about if I bring it back to you on those days when your other customers need it. I shouldn't have it for very long anyway."

"All right, but let's us agree that you rent her by the day." He twirled his toothpick between his fingers. "What ya figuring to pay?"

I looked across the yard at the sad little hatchback and its lack of paint. "Does eight dollars work for you?"

"Yeah, that's fair. You're gonna have to take her with the dents. I've had no time to smooth 'em out."

"That's fine." After all, I was the one who had made those dents while doing a very poor imitation of a stunt driver as I fled the bad guys in Los Angeles. Since I was obligated to pay for the repair, it was fine by me if the dents stayed. It wasn't like it could make the car look any worse.

Sliding the toothpick between his molars, Cal stuck out his hand. "We got a deal."

I grabbed it, feeling his strength under the callouses and grit. "Yes, we do."

CHAPTER FIVE

On the ride back from our visit with Ruthie, I promised Dori I would follow up with Malachi to see if there had been any progress in running down the cartel, so when leaving Cal's yard in my *new* hatchback I pulled over to call him, thinking since it was after hours in New York he'd never pick up. To my first surprise, he did, on the second ring. And to my second, he was talkative, for him anyway.

No. They weren't much closer to finding Carrick. The gang members they arrested in New York and L.A. were apparently far more afraid of their boss than being sent to prison, so they weren't talking. Malachi did tell me that the D.A. was negotiating with the defense attorneys for Martin and Brandon Moran, in whose house I had been imprisoned with six trafficked laborers. As witnesses, the Morans were invaluable to the prosecution's case. Their knowledge also put them in a lot of danger. Carrick no doubt wanted them dead.

Malachi also implied that Carrick would be a lot better off if Dori and I never had a chance to testify either. Comforting thought.

I told Malachi I didn't know how much good that testimony from Martin Moran was going to be to the D.A.'s case, since he had been drunk the majority of time the laborers were locked up in his house and he claimed he thought they were renters. His son Brandon had participated in their confinement, however, and was on a fast track to ruining his life. He hadn't seemed like a bad kid to me, so I was relieved to hear that Malachi caught him before Carrick did. Brandon had been fearful of retribution if he left the gang, for good reason, but I liked his chances much better with the courts than the criminals. I was hopeful that after all the dust settled someone might be able to help him find some direction.

One of the things I was most concerned about was the fate of the trafficking victims. Malachi said it was such a complex issue, requiring so many services–legal, medical, social–he wasn't sure of their status.

I asked him to call me if he heard anything at all. My nerves were on edge from fear of being tracked down by the cartel, and Dori was anxious to get back to L.A. He said he would keep us updated and reassured me that despite the gang's desire to silence us, there was very little chance of them showing up in Harmony.

When signing off, a hint of Malachi's Irish accent came through, which reminded me of his cover identity when I first met him in the Bronx–Irish singer and collector of spandex-skirted women. I was to tell Dori, he said, that he still needed convincing about why she was in such a hurry to return to Southern California when it was *oh so much lovelier* in the East. I agreed to forward the message, thinking it sounded to me like he was looking forward to having Dori make her argument for L.A. in person and in a dimly lit room. Although, I doubted Dori would show up in a skirt hiked up to her fanny.

Disconnecting from my call, I continued down Main Street and nosed my car into a space in front of Dusty's Diner–I needed a buffalo Bolognese fix. I was going to order my dinner to go, however, as Mr. B and Alice had been left alone on Noah's ranch all day.

Patrick was sitting at the counter in his usual spot when I walked in. Luke was at a far booth, his head in a video game, and Dori was refilling coffee cups at one of only three tables with diners. I slid onto the stool next to Patrick to wait for Dori to take my order. During my previous stay in Harmony, I discovered that Patrick's passion was solving cold cases. Sadly, the one involving the deaths of the two girls from Samuel's polygamist cult was one of them. With that type of work, there couldn't be many happy endings. The best Patrick could hope for was closure, which was apparently enough to keep him at it. Swiveling my stool in his direction, I decided to find out if he had any he was working on at the moment. "Any new cold cases?" I asked.

"There was a murder up at the Bliss Mine several years back, or at least they suspect it was murder. It was never really proven. I thought I'd take a look into that. I've been wanting to get up that way anyway, do a little hiking."

"Where's the Bliss Mine?"

"Just outside the Dixie Forest, a little over an hour from here."

"I like to hike," Luke said, having overheard us as he got up to clear a few plates and set them behind the counter. "And, I want to study forensic science."

"And the Aurora Borealis. And Alaska." I smiled at Luke. "How do you know about forensics?"

"My teacher in Los Angeles told us about it. Can I go with you to the Bliss Mine, Deputy Crane?"

"What are you all so busy talking about?" Dori joined the group. Noticing that there were still dishes on one of the tables, she said, "Luke, you need to finish your job."

"Deputy Crane is going to the Bliss Mine to investigate a murder." He ignored her command. "And, I want to go with him. Please, please can I go with him?"

"You know that begging will get you nowhere. Clear the dishes, please."

"But ..."

"Now." Dori frowned at him.

Stooped shouldered, Luke walked away.

"I wouldn't mind taking him along," Patrick said.

"Really?"

"I'd be happy to. I'm planning to go up there on Sunday."

"That'd be great. He's been so bored since we got here. He needs to get back to his program and his school in L.A. If Malachi and his bunch don't catch those guys by next week, I'm out of here, I swear. I'd rather take my chances in L.A. than lose all the progress we made there."

"I talked to Malachi," I said.

"And?"

"And, nothing. But, he promised to keep us updated."

"Great." She frowned.

"He had a message for you."

"Oh?"

Feigning my best Irish accent, I said, "I'd be likin' it if you'd tell me why you want to live in Los Angeles when it's oh so lovely in the East." Dropping the accent, I continued, "And, I think he'd prefer you explain in person–just the two of you."

"I doubt that."

"I don't."

"I'll take my check now," Patrick said, looking disinterested in the turn the conversation had taken.

"And, I'll take a buffalo Bolognese to go, please," I said, "When you get a minute."

"Oh, sure." Dori reached into her skirt pocket for her pad, tore the top sheet off and scribbled my order on the next one. "I really appreciate your offer to take Luke with you on Sunday." She handed Patrick his tab.

"No problem."

"I get to go!" Luke overheard Dori's last remark from where he was lurking within earshot.

"Yeah, but only if you don't pester Deputy Crane and me with a thousand questions between now and then."

"But, we need to make a plan."

"Yes, we do, Luke. How about you come to my office on Saturday morning at ten, and we'll work on it."

"I can do that. Yes. I'll come to your office at ten on Saturday morning."

Patrick stood up from his stool after leaving cash on the counter. "I gotta get back to the office. I'll see you on Saturday, Luke."

"See you!" he said.

As I bounced along Noah's road in the fading dusk, I remembered that I meant to ask Cal about the hatchback's shock absorbers–as in–were there any? I really needed to find more editing work if I was ever going to afford to move up from a sub-compact wreck of a car.

I didn't see any signs of Mr. Bumbles as I pulled up next to the motorhome, which we had parked close enough to connect to an electrical outlet on the porch. I figured Mr. B was probably hanging out with Noah's dog, Trudy, although I was not too sure how much tolerance she had for his laid-back lifestyle. She was an Australian Shepherd, quick of foot and mind. Mr. B, not so much.

The minute I closed the car door, buffalo Bolognese in hand, my hound appeared around the back of the house and headed my direction in high gear, which for him is a slow trot. I could always count on his nose for a good meal to bring him back to me. Only I wasn't sharing this one. He was going to have to settle for kibble a la mode.

Trudy followed right behind him, and Noah after her–a welcoming committee. It was nice.

"Honey, I'm home," I smiled, making a joke to cover the awkwardness I felt at *moving in* with Noah.

"Long day at the office?" Noah smiled also.

"Exhausting!"

"Dinner's just about done."

"Let me loosen my tie and get Mr. Bumbles to bring me my slippers and I'll be right there." I thought he was still kidding.

"I made lasagna."

Realizing he was serious I held up the box from Dusty's, feeling even more awkward. "I bought dinner for myself. Buffalo Bolognese."

"That works. We've got an Italian theme going. I'll take it in and warm it up."

"You don't have to do that. I've got a microwave."

"What would you have us do, Sydney, eat at our tables by ourselves, wondering what the other person is doing?"

Jeez, he knew how to cut through the crap. "No."

"Good, then do what you have to do in the motorhome, and come on over." He put his hand out and waited for me to give him the box.

"Okay." I was still hesitant, but finally handed it to him.

"Cheer up." He grinned. "It's not a penance. You'll have fun, trust me."

"That's what I'm afraid of." I rolled my eyes.

He chuckled and shook his head. "I'll put the outside lights on so you can find your way over. And you're welcome to bring Mr. Bumbles along. Don't get lost."

"I won't."

I don't know why I was reluctant to have dinner with Noah. Why was I so guarded? I wanted to be with him. I could tell by the quickening of my pulse as I raised my hand to knock on his door. Mr. B was excited too, his tail shifting to high gear when he heard Trudy announce my arrival with a few loud yips.

Noah pulled the door open, holding a wine opener and wearing a khaki-colored apron with *FFA Member* written across it. Trudy stood at his feet.

"Well, hey, Martha Stewart. I didn't know you flew," I said.

"What?" He followed my eyes to the words on his apron.

"FFA."

"Yeah?"

"The flying association."

"That's F*AA*. This is Future Farmers of America." His eyes twinkled. "The only wings they deal with are on chickens."

"Oh. My bad." That was stupid. I should have known, with more cows in the area than people. So much for my attempt at humor.

"Come on in. It's cold out there."

"Thanks." I stepped past him into the entry. The aroma of Italian seasoning laced with smoldering firewood embraced me like a warm hug.

"I was just about to grab some wine from the cellar." He gestured for us to head down the hall to the kitchen.

"You have a wine cellar?" I didn't remember seeing one on any of my previous visits.

"No. I have a cellar where I keep wine among boxes of stuff that needs going through. Go ahead and make yourself at home." He disappeared through a door at the back of the kitchen and down a set of stairs. I sat down at the banquette and Mr. B and Trudy settled down beside me.

"If you ever want to give up cattle ranching, you really could make a living as a chef." I scooped the last bite of lasagna from my plate. "This is, what, three meals I owe you now?"

"At least." He picked up our plates and walked them over to the counter.

"For your sake, I'll be paying you back at a restaurant of your choice. Have I mentioned I'm a really bad cook?"

"No. But, I guessed it from the contents of your cupboards and fridge."

"What? Fritos and yogurt don't count as gourmet food?"

"Not really."

"I do a mean job of dishwashing, though." I stood and joined him at the sink. "If you hand me that sponge and take a seat, I'll have them done in a jiffy."

"Nah. We'll do them together."

"Okay." I shrugged.

I never thought of washing dishes as an intimate act, but somehow with Noah it was. We chatted over nothings as he washed and I dried, and those minutes of nothings connected us more than any conversation we'd ever had. And here I thought that forming deep bonds required the exchange of our inmost thoughts, when maybe all that was needed was the unguarded pleasure of the tiniest gestures. Was that the secret to those long marriages you read about in the paper–seventy years of exchanging nothings over morning coffee and dirty saucepans? Amazing.

That evening with Noah was as if we'd stepped through a portal to the 1950s. We played dominos, listened to music on the radio, made popcorn. The dogs completed the picture, curled up on a hearthrug next to a blazing fire. I kept thinking June Cleaver was going to walk in wearing her pearls and a lace-trimmed apron, carrying a tray full of homemade cookies.

When the night moved along to the bedroom, however, we were entirely in the present. Moment by long intoxicating moment, our lovemaking was both tender and powerful–an act of love. It left me breathless and content. Was I finally ready to accept that contentment? Was I finally ready to accept that I couldn't control every bend in this journey I'd been on for several months and several thousand miles? Could losing my bearings could be a good thing?

Yes.

The scenery had changed. And finally, I was ready to do the same.

CHAPTER SIX

I'd been elected to drive Ruthie and her baby to her former home for a visit, because there wasn't enough room in the cab of V.A.'s truck for all of them. We got an early start, since V.A. had clients later that morning.

On my way to pick her up, I called Vincent Bettencourt, the man who ran the anti-trafficking office in New York. I wanted to make sure he was okay with polygamy as a topic for their newsletter. As an advocate for the oppressed, in whatever form, he was open to the idea. He told me that in order to meet the deadline, however, I'd have to email a draft to him in the next two weeks. Pressure–but I was okay with it. When I hung up I felt a genuine rush of excitement at the prospect of writing the article–an enthusiasm for work I hadn't experienced in a very long time.

When Ruthie and I arrived at the house formerly occupied by fugitive and all-around really bad guy, Samuel Vaullie, we joined Dori and V.A., who were waiting for us by the gate. Making our way up the front walk, we couldn't possibly have gone unnoticed by the inhabitants, for Remy had picked that time to be heard–by everyone in a five-mile radius–she was crying so hard. Ruthie had chosen to leave her in the infant car seat, and she was not happy about it. When we finally reached the stoop, Ruthie set her down and began undoing the safety harness. V.A. pushed the doorbell and we all stood casting our eyes between the door and inconsolable Remy.

Two minutes went by, then three, and no one came to the door. Great. Helen, the woman who I assumed was wife number one of Samuel Vaullie because of her superior attitude in our previous encounters, had tried to bar us from coming in when Ruthie was in labor with Remy. It seemed as if she was still playing at that same game, even with Ruthie, who was part of her group—albeit only because they were married to the same man. I hoped. It would take on a whole lot viler meaning if Helen turned out to be Ruthie's aunt or something.

Ringing the bell again then knocking loudly on the door, V.A. stepped off the porch and began walking along the front of the house, peering into the narrow windows. The first time I'd seen the place I thought it looked like a prison and I hadn't changed my mind.

"There are lights on." V.A. rejoined us. "Try the doorknob." She nodded at Dori.

Dori jiggled it and shook her head. "Locked."

"Okay. I'm going around back. There's definitely someone home," V.A. said.

"Why don't you try the shushing thing," Dori said to Ruthie, who was now holding a wailing Remy close to her chest.

Ruthie cradled Remy in the crook of her arm, bounced her and shushed into her face. Although she continued to cry it seemed like she was running out of steam.

"Where in the heck are they?" I asked Dori when several more minutes had passed.

"I don't know." Dori glanced over at Ruthie, who was looking anxious. The poor thing. Who leaves a crying baby and her young mother standing out in the cold?

After hugging our arms to our chests awhile longer, now thoroughly chilled, the door finally opened. It was Helen, with V.A. standing right behind her, almost a head taller.

"Hello, Ruthie," Helen said quietly, her face revealing no emotion.

"Hello, Mother Helen," Ruthie's voice took on an unnaturally high pitch.

"Come on in before you freeze," V.A. urged us from over the top of Helen's head.

Helen moved aside to let us pass and we all squished into the small entryway. "Let's go into the kitchen," V.A. said, when no offer came from Helen as to where she planned to have us go. From her stiff stance and reluctance to speak, it seemed that our visit was under protest.

When we walked into the large utilitarian kitchen a woman named Agnes was standing there, her hands folded in front of her. She had been at Remy's birth and at the hospital where Ruthie was taken after Doctor Schrum almost killed her with his incompetence.

"Why don't you all sit down," V.A. nodded at the large kitchen table, acting the hostess. "I'll help you make some tea if you have some," she said to Agnes.

"We do," Agnes said, only after Helen gave her a slight nod.

After we gathered around the table, Ruthie removed the baby's hooded jacket and smiling shyly at Helen, said, "This is Remy." Big-eyed, round-cheeked Remy was looking much happier now that she was no longer trussed up for winter.

That sweet face didn't soften Helen's heart one bit. "Yes, I see that," was all she said. No comments like, *she's beautiful* or *she's got your mouth*, out of that woman. What a bitch.

"How has everyone been?" Ruthie looked from Helen to Agnes, who was pouring hot water into cups.

"Fine," they both said, with no further comment.

"I'd love to see Angela. I've really missed her. Is she upstairs?"

I noticed a look of fear cross Agnes's eyes before she covered it with a sudden interest in serving us the tea. "Do you take milk or sugar?" She pretended not to hear Ruthie's question. Had anyone else noticed Agnes's distress? Dori was busy draping her sweater on the back of her chair, and V.A. was removing tea bags from the cups, so I wasn't sure.

"A little milk, please," Dori said.

"I'll put some on the table for everyone." Agnes turned back to the kitchen counter.

"Has she been a healthy baby?" Helen asked Ruthie with warmth in her tone, also ignoring the question about Angela. Why the sudden change?

"Oh, yes, very." Ruthie picked Remy up under her arms and touched her feet to the tabletop. "See how she can put her weight on her legs? The doctor says she's really strong."

"May I hold her?" Helen asked.

Ruthie's eyes lit up with the older woman's sudden interest in Remy. "Of course!" She handed her to Helen.

Helen set Remy's bottom on the edge of the table and studied her face. "She looks like a good baby. Does she sleep through the night yet?"

As Ruthie answered her and they continued to talk it looked the cozy domestic scene, but I wasn't buying it.

"Where did you say Angela was?" I looked straight at Agnes just as she was setting the cup of tea down in front of me.

"Um ..." She turned her eyes from mine and concentrated on her hands.

"She's gone down to Magdalena's for her math lessons," Mother Helen answered for Agnes.

"She has?" Ruthie was genuinely surprised. "But, that's your job, Agnes."

"Uh, well ..." Agnes walked over to the counter to pick up another cup. "We've been trading off some."

"Oh?" Ruthie looked perplexed.

"We've all had to take on additional responsibilities," Helen said, a statement clearly designed to make Ruthie feel guilty for not being there.

It backfired on her when V.A. asked, "Samuel leave you high and dry?"

Helen handed Remy back to Ruthie and raised her chin. "It's been a trial, but we're managing."

"Has Samuel contacted you?" V.A. looked from Helen to Agnes, who was back at the table. Again, fear flashed across her face. This time Dori and V.A. caught it too.

"He has! Hasn't he, Agnes?" Dori put her hand on Agnes's arm as she set a cup down in front of her. "Sit down, Agnes. Now. If you two know something about Samuel's whereabouts, you need to tell us and, more importantly, Deputy Crane."

"Do not say a word, Agnes," Helen warned.

"You'd protect that man?" Dori slapped her hand hard on the table. "He's responsible for the deaths of Gloria and Joannie and he almost killed Ruthie!"

"But ..." Agnes started to say.

"I told you, don't talk!" Helen said.

"Go ahead and follow Helen's orders, Agnes," V.A. said, "and see where that gets you. If he was here only for a few minutes, you could be accused of harboring a fugitive. Do you want to go to jail, Agnes?"

Agnes looked from V.A. to Helen, alarm building on her face.

Ruthie had been sitting quietly patting Remy's back the whole time. "Don't protect him," she finally said, holding Agnes's eyes in hers. "If you ever got out of this place, you'd know it's wrong. *He's* wrong. He is so wrong." She pushed her chair back, stood up and came around the table to stand in front of Agnes. "He made me marry him. I was fifteen!" Her voice rose. Remy started wriggling in her arms. "That was wrong! Wrong! Wrong! Wrong! Don't you see?" Ruthie stifled back a sob.

"Here, let me take her." I held my arms out to Ruthie. Remy was working her way into a fuss, sensing her mother's agitation.

"If you know where Samuel is, you need to tell," Dori said, as Ruthie passed Remy to me.

"Agnes!" Helen said, a sharp warning in her voice.

"No!" Ruthie said, the cruelty she'd suffered for years finally surfacing. "No, Mother Helen! You do not get to stop Agnes from telling the truth. You went along with everything he did! You covered everything up, just like him. It was *your* job to stop him and you didn't. You're just as evil as him!"

Ruthie was shaking by then and her eyes welled with tears. V.A. walked over, put her arm around her and said evenly to Helen, "Every word Ruthie said is true. It's time both of you do the right thing." She looked hard at Agnes. "If Helen doesn't have the courage to say something, Agnes, you need to."

With all eyes on her, Agnes stared at her hands wrapped around the cup in front of her. "He's up in the forest somewhere hiding out with some other men." Her voice was so soft we could barely hear her.

Helen sighed.

"And, he has An ..."

"No!" Helen snapped.

"Angela?" I looked from Helen to Agnes. I knew there was something going on with Angela!

"Look at me, Agnes," V.A. commanded. "Does Samuel have Angela?"

Lifting her head and with tears beginning to flow down her face, she whispered, "Yes."

"When did he take her?" V.A. asked.

"Two days ago."

"Two days ago. My God!" Dori grabbed Agnes's arms. "He's with other men–probably dangerous criminals–and you didn't report it? What in the hell is the matter with you?" She got right in her face.

Ruthie wrapped her arms around her middle, rocked back and forth, and whispered, "No, no, no, no, no."

"He's not going to harm her." Helen scowled at us. "She's his daughter. He loves her."

"Right! Like he loved Gloria, and Joannie, and Ruthie!" Dori spat out. "You're full of shit, Helen, and you deserve to rot in hell beside him!"

"I'm calling Deputy Crane," V.A. said, and we're going to sit here with you until he arrives. Then you're going to tell him everything you know. Is that clear? Agnes? Helen?"

Agnes nodded her head. Helen just looked away from her.

Patrick arrived a short time later, but didn't learn much from his interrogation of the women. All Samuel had told them was that he was living in the mountains with two other men, raising money so he could make his way across the border into Mexico. Apparently there were a few groups of Mormons down there that still practiced polygamy.

His rationale for taking Angela was that with her along law enforcement would be far less likely to approach him with guns drawn. And he had assured Mother Helen there would be plenty of women in Mexico happy to have Angela as part of their family. Insane. And sickening!

Dori was so disgusted with Mother Helen and Agnes she wouldn't even look at them as we left. Before she and V.A. took off, she asked me to come early to round dance practice because there was something she needed to discuss with me. It was a vague request and I got the feeling that was because V.A. was standing there.

When I returned Ruthie and Remy to the ranch, I pulled Miriam aside and let her know what had transpired. She assured me that she would look after Ruthie and do her best to calm her fears about Angela. She said she believed that despite all Samuel had done he would keep her safe. I doubted it.

CHAPTER SEVEN

When I returned to Noah's ranch, there was no sign of him. I figured he spent his days roaming the range, or whatever cowboys do. Mr. Bumbles and Alice were waiting for me inside the RV. Or rather, they were both sound asleep in their favorite spots, Alice on my bed, and Mr. B next to the dinette. I had left him inside because it was a cold day and I wasn't confident that if *he* started roaming the range he'd be back before nightfall. There were way too many critters and smells to keep him sniffing and chasing. After a quick lunch and short walk with Mr. B so he could do his business, I headed back to Harmony.

Dori was just finishing up with the last of the lunch stragglers when I arrived at Dusty's. Signaling for me to take a seat in a booth, she came over in a few minutes with a cup of coffee for me.

"So, what's up?" I said after she settled herself across from me, pulled her long dark hair out of its band and draped it behind her back.

"Samuel." She took a sip of her own coffee and set it down. "I don't think we can wait for the sheriff's department to find him. He could be long gone to Mexico with Angela by then."

"But, what can *we* do? We don't know where he is." I wrapped my hands around my warm cup.

"I think *I* do." Dori stared at me.

"How?"

"You know how Agnes first said that Samuel was hiding out in the forest and then later said it was the mountains? There are a lot of mountains in this part of Utah that are just rock–no trees, or very few. And remember how we saw Samuel just outside of St. George?"

"Yeah."

"Well, just above there is the Dixie Forest–mountains with pine forests. There are a lot of vacation homes up there that people don't use all the time. I'll bet they're in one of them."

"But, isn't it a large area? How would you know where to look?"

"It's not as big as you think. The homes are clustered along just a few roads."

"Why don't you tell Deputy Crane about your hunch? Let him check it out."

"No. The minute he'd show up in his car and uniform the word would get out and they'd be out of there."

"So, what are you proposing to do?"

"Crane is taking Luke up to the Bliss Mine on Sunday, which should take all day, so I won't have to worry about him. I'll tell Dusty I can't work that day and then the two of us can go up to the Dixie Forest and nose around. If we do find out which cabin he's in, then we'll tell Crane."

I hesitated. It sounded wacky–and dangerous. "Isn't there snow up there this time of year?"

"Yeah, but that can be our cover. We can pretend like we're out on a snowshoe hike."

"A snowshoe hike? I don't have any in my closet." I stared at her like she was nuts.

"I'll get you some."

"I don't know, Dori. Samuel's a violent man and who knows what the creeps he's with are like."

"Okay, then, how 'bout this?" She tapped her finger on the table. "I'll make you a deal. If you take me up there, you can have all the way up to the mountain and back to ask me questions about polygamy for that article you told me you're writing."

I glanced out the window as a car pulled up in front of Dusty's then looked back at Dori. "Okay, I'll go up there with you, but not just because of the article." I leaned toward her across the table. "I'll do it because I know you well enough that I have no doubt you'll go up there with or without me. Am I right?"

She shrugged her shoulders.

"I'm right."

As we finished our conversation a few women came in and started pushing the tables to the side, clearing a large space in the dining room under the direction of Dusty.

"Time for round dance practice." Dori stood up from the booth.

"Are you staying for it?"

"I might for a few minutes, but I've got to work tonight too. I want to get out of here for awhile. I already know most of the steps anyway."

"You're that good?"

"Sure. It's fun!"

"Is it a Harmony rule or something? All citizens of the town *must round dance.*"

"Yes, I believe it is." Dori smiled. "Or, at least when you grow up without music and dancing and laughter the way Luke and I did you wouldn't want to live any place where it wasn't one."

"I'll make sure to add that to my deal-breaker list for my dream town." I smiled back.

V.A. came through Dusty's door, followed by several other women and a smattering of men. Cal was one of them. Cal?

After the floor had been cleared, a short rotund man with a hairline that started well back of his forehead set a small sound system down on top of the counter and started fiddling with knobs.

"Who's that?" I asked Dori.

"Avery Smith. He's our cuer."

"Cuer? What's that?"

"He's the one who calls out the steps to the dancers, kinda like a caller in square dancing. Only in round dancing the cuer reads from a cue sheet that has all the steps choreographed and written down."

"Okay. I guess I get that. How many different steps are we talking about?"

"There's quite a few, but round dancing is based on smooth and Latin rhythms, so if you know how to waltz, foxtrot, cha-cha, dances like that, you'll pick it up easy. Avery usually keeps it pretty basic."

I looked at Dori, who was dressed in her usual variation on black, thinking that the last thing I ever expected was for her to be an expert on dance rhythms. But then, she wasn't like any other twenty-something I'd ever met. "I don't think it's going to be that easy for me. The one and only time I ever ballroom danced was in a college class I took as an elective. I don't remember a thing."

"It'll come back to you, Missy," V.A. said, having overheard our conversation.

"Okay. Partner up, everybody," Avery said through his microphone. "Time to get started."

"Partner up?" I looked from Dori to V.A.

"Yeah," V.A. said. "It's a couples dance, done in a circle that moves counter-clockwise."

Looking around the room, I watched everyone pair up with little regard for keeping it to boy-girl couples. There weren't enough boys anyway.

"We'll come on, Missy." V.A. nodded toward the circle that was forming and started over there.

I guess I found my partner. I looked back at Dori, who grinned. "You not coming?"

"No. I'll brush up on a few steps from here, and then I'm leaving."

Fortunately, I wasn't the only dancer who needed a major review. And even more critical, Avery was a patient man. He took us through the rhythms and steps very slowly. I only crunched V.A.'s toes a few times, which she thought was more funny than painful, reacting with her fog-horn laugh. I was pretty sure it was the first time I had ever danced with a woman, so it felt a bit odd at first. In observing the other dancers, however, it was obvious they subscribed to the *dance like nobody's watching* philosophy. They were having a blast! This was a whole new concept for me, who hailed from the land where people watching was a driving force and mirrors were everyone's favorite toys.

We had just moved on to the Latin dances, when Cal's girlfriend Lou walked in. Like the few other men, Cal had been taking turns with the ladies, and at that juncture was facing his partner and holding both her hands.

Lou marched over to the two of them and stood with her hands on her hips.

"Hello, Honeybunch," Cal said. "You made it. We was just startin' in to a cha-cha."

"Good. I like a cha-cha." She stared deliberately at Cal's partner.

Squirming like she'd been caught naked in the middle of Main Street, the woman dropped her hands from Cal's. She stepped out of the circle and hurried over to the smattering of people who were watching from the sidelines.

"Why is everyone so afraid of Cal's girlfriend?" I whispered to V.A.

"Not everyone." There was an edge to V.A.'s voice. Interesting.

The music had started back up, so I didn't ask her to elaborate. I probably wouldn't have gotten an answer anyway. V.A. wasn't much of a sharer.

After an afternoon of practice, I felt pretty good about holding my own at the round dance, or rather, with only a few of them *Dancing With the Stars* candidates, I figured I couldn't be any worse than the rest.

When Dusty's had been reassembled into a diner, I grabbed a quick dinner and headed back to Noah's ranch. Riding down the highway, focused on the round dance practice, I found myself smiling. It had been fun. And fun was something I needed more of in my life, after the serious turn it took with the trafficking gang. There was nothing like a little camaraderie and laughter to fire up the endorphins. I was actually looking forward to Saturday night.

About two miles before the turnoff to Noah's ranch, the first headlights I'd seen since leaving Harmony approached at a fast speed. Still jumpy from worrying about the whereabouts of Carrick, I concentrated on keeping my car on the far right side of my lane. As the headlights neared, the other driver suddenly took a sharp left in front of me. Pressing hard on my brakes, I yelled, "Idiot!" And as I watched the car disappear down the gravel lane, I realized it was a sedan and it looked very familiar. Samuel! It had to be! But no, what would he be doing out here? And why would he risk coming so close to town?

I could follow him and find out. No! I gripped the steering wheel. The past few months had frayed my nerves and made me paranoid. It would be nuts to follow that car down a dark road when there were thousands of sedans in Utah that looked just like it. No, I needed to tootle on back to Noah's ranch and forget about it. But, of course, I wouldn't. I had already started plotting a mission down that road.

When I pulled up next to the motorhome, I looked over at the barn to see it ablaze in lights. What was Noah doing? Stepping out of the car and tugging my sweater tight to my torso, I made my way around his house to see what was going on.

As I entered the cavernous space, I was shocked to find it almost completely empty of everything but a stack of hay bales. Noah was up on a ladder hammering something into a beam. When I walked toward him, Mr. Bumbles and Trudy trotted over to greet me.

"I let him out of the motorhome. Hope you don't mind." Noah dropped his arms and looked down at Mr. B, who was standing at my feet alongside Trudy, waiting for attention.

"No. That's great!" I obliged Mr. B by scratching him behind his long silky ears, then patted Trudy. "He was probably getting bored."

"Do you think he *gets bored*?" Noah smiled.

"Not so long as there's a good spot to plop down." I smiled back. "Where'd everything go?" I peered beyond him to the massive workbench I'd seen on the tour Noah gave me of his place the first time I visited. Even that had been cleared of most of its tools and paint cans.

"I moved the heavy equipment out back and stored the rest away. The decorating crew is coming first thing in the morning."

"So, people are really into it."

"Oh yeah, but you probably found that out at practice this afternoon. How'd it go?"

"Great! Everyone seemed to enjoy themselves, except for maybe the woman who Lou caught dancing with Cal. What's with Lou, anyway? And why is everyone so intimidated by her? She's worse than Genevieve."

"She can be territorial, but I wouldn't lump her in with Genevieve."

"No, I suppose not. Lou's hair color definitely didn't come in a bottle and I doubt any of her body parts are made of silicone." Oops. Did I say that?

Noah refrained from commenting on my snide remark. "So, how'd you do?" he asked, after climbing down from the ladder.

"How'd I do?"

"At round dancing?"

"Pretty well, I think."

"Show me."

"What, here?" I looked around.

"Sure."

"But, there's no music and no cuer."

"That's okay." He set the hammer on the ladder rung and took my hands in his. "I'll call out the steps. Let's start with a waltz."

"Okay?" I frowned at him. "You didn't tell me you moonlighted as a dance instructor."

His eyes twinkling, he called out the first step and nudged me forward.

"What song are we dancing to?" I asked, as I failed to pick up on the waltz rhythm. "If I'm going to do this, I need to have a song in my head."

"Okay, then." He hesitated as he thought. "How about *Are You Lonesome Tonight*, The Elvis Presley song. Do you know it?" He whistled the first few bars in a sweet crystal tone that bounced to the rafters and showered down on us.

"Wow. That was beautiful. My dad was a good whistler. He'd always whistle up our front walk, so we'd know he was home before he came through the door. Although he was more of a Beach Boys than an Elvis guy." By the time I finished the sentence, the beginning of an ache started forming in my chest. It had to have been the combination of the melancholy mood of the Elvis song and the memory of my dad. Suddenly interested in straightening my sweater, I looked away from him, dropped my hands from his and tugged on the hem.

Feeling his arm around my shoulder, I looked back over and Noah gave it a squeeze. No comment, just an *I get it* gesture. There was a lot to be said for a man who knew when words were not necessary.

"Okay. You ready?"

"Sure."

Grabbing my hands and whistling the first notes of the song once again, Noah led us away from the ladder and called out the first step. As we moved to the notes of *Are You Lonesome Tonight* playing in our heads, Noah continued to cue the steps one after the other. Patient when I couldn't remember a move, he'd stop and walk me through it until I got it right. After a while, I was finally more confident. Dancing with Noah felt graceful and natural–and sexy, definitely sexy–a term I wouldn't have otherwise associated with round *or* square dancing.

Every time a step brought us close together, my eyes would lock on those blue ones of his or that hair curling down his neck. It took every bit of willpower I had to focus on the dance. My attraction to him was that powerful.

"How'd you learn all this, and why?" I asked, thankful for the distraction of having to concentrate as he demonstrated a more complicated step. I wasn't sure how long I could keep from jumping into his arms–not a pretty sight when your legs are as long as mine.

"I think I told you my folks love to dance. It was something we grew up with."

"And novels like *The Scarlet Letter*, did you grow up with those too?"

"There have always been stacks of books yay high," he spread his hands far apart, "all over my parents' house. And my mother read stories aloud to my sister, father, and me clear into my high school years."

"She did? I thought you'd have been too busy with your friends cutting cattle or climbing rocks, or whatever ranch boys do for fun."

"Cutting cattle? Where'd you come up with that?"

"Cal."

"And you know what it means?"

"Yeah."

"I can teach you that too, if you like." His eyes danced.

"No. I'm good." The sight of Lou slicing off a calf's testicles flashed in front of my eyes.

"If you change your mind, you let me know." He reached for my hands.

"I'll do that." I smiled, feeling the warmth of his callouses, our fingers entwined. "Hey, Noah," I didn't move when he started into the next step.

"Yeah." He studied my eyes.

"Your childhood sounds like it was pretty wonderful and your parents have a good marriage, right?"

He nodded.

"So, why haven't *you* ever married?" There, I put it out there–something I'd been wondering since I first met him.

Instead of stumbling over the question or getting defensive as I expected a lot of men would do, he didn't even blink. He answered straight up. "Never found a woman who was the right fit."

"You mean, who shared your interests?"

"No. I mean in my arms."

"Literally?"

"Yeah."

"Well, that's really Prince Charming of you. How does it work? You have your footman scour the land for a woman whose hug circumference fits your exact requirement?"

"No, I just do this." He closed the gap between us, lifted my hands around his neck then wrapped his arms around my waist and pressed his body into mine. I laid my head on his shoulder as he ran his hands up and down my back. We stayed like that for a long time, with me wondering all the while if *I* was that right fit. Instead of answering my unasked question, he began softly whistling the melody of *Are You Lonesome Tonight* once again, gently gliding us across the floor to its haunting rhythm.

Later that night as we drifted off to sleep, nestled together like two spoons from the same set of silverware, he still hadn't answered my question. As for my own answer, I decided to dream on it.

CHAPTER EIGHT

When I awakened enough to notice that the sun was well up, I also realized that Mr. B, Trudy, and Noah had left the room. After one last cat stretch under the warm covers, I got out of bed. Sliding my socks on, I wrapped myself in my sweater to ward off the chill in the house. Noah liked to keep the thermostat on the Arctic setting.

After a quick run to the bathroom, I decided to see if Noah was in the kitchen. It was still early enough that he should be there, and if not I could use a cup of coffee, even if it was just to warm my hands.

When I stepped through the door to the kitchen, I stopped short, horrified. Four people were seated at the banquette, and two of them were Miriam and Odelia. Her back to me, Odelia was in a kitchen chair with her walker beside her. Next to her was a woman with short brown hair. Facing me, Miriam was sitting next to a man with sun-tanned skin and silver-gray hair. They both looked over at me when they saw my movement, their eyes shifting from my face to my bare legs. Following their stares, I was just as shocked as they were to discover that I hadn't bothered to put on any pants. When I looked back up, I caught sight of Noah out of the corner of my eye. He was standing next to the counter, a coffee pot in his hand. Noticing Odelia's and the other woman's heads start to turn, I stepped back and yanked the door shut before they could see me.

Shit! Shit! Shit! Hurrying to the bedroom, my heart pounding, and my face on fire, I threw on my clothes and shoes then stood there. What was I going to do? There was no way I was going back into that kitchen and face those people!

Walking over to the window, I pulled back the curtain and looked down. It wasn't too far a drop, maybe eight or ten feet. Unlocking it, I raised the sash and stuck my head out. My first thought was that leaping from Noah's window was a piece of cake compared to kicking my way out of the Moran's attic in the Bronx. I still had a scar from that escapade.

Sizing up the opening, I thought if I went out feet first I could hang on to the frame and drop to the ground.

"Leaving so soon?"

Startled at hearing a voice, I jumped and hit my head on the window sash. "Ouch!" Rubbing it, I turned to face Noah.

"So, you've decided to take up fleeing through windows as a hobby?" He was grinning, and I wasn't happy about it!

"No!"

"Then what exactly are you doing?"

"Going to the motorhome."

"My house has doors."

"I know." I continued to rub my head.

"So, why don't you use one? But before then you should come into the kitchen and meet my parents."

"Your parents? Oh my, God! Why didn't you tell me they were going to be here this morning?"

"They just dropped by. They're helping decorate the barn."

"Dropped by?"

"Yeah. Dropped by. Don't Californians ever drop by?"

"No! At least not ones from L.A. They text to say they're coming and they're usually about a half hour late because there was traffic on the 405!"

He laughed. Laughed!

"It's not funny! Your father and Miriam saw me half naked!"

"Miriam has seen you in a robe before."

"That doesn't count. They know I slept here!"

"So. We're grownups. Now, come out and meet them. They're going to wonder what happened to me."

"No. I can't. I'm too embarrassed."

"So, you're just going to spend the rest of the day in here?"

"No. I'll come out when they leave. Or, there's always the window." I looked over my shoulder and when I looked back at him even I had to grin at the ridiculousness of my escape plan.

"So, come on." He nodded at the door.

"No, really. I can't. Won't. You go visit. Do you think they'll see me if I use your front door?"

"Not likely." He sighed. "I'll let you off for now, but then you need to show your face in the barn this morning. I want you to meet my folks and the committee could use your help."

"All right." I dropped my shoulders. I was going to have to meet his parents anyway, since they were apparently attending the round dance. I may as well get it over with sooner rather than later. "Can I come back and use your shower after they go? I don't want your dad to have to see me like this a second time." I lifted the sides of my hair.

Walking over, he wrapped his arms around my waist. "There's nothing wrong with *this*." He lowered his head and kissed my neck. "Or this, or this." He continued kissing me up to my earlobe and nibbled on it. "You're one crazy lady." He pulled back.

"You think so?" I shrugged my shoulders and followed him out of the room, down the hall and to the front door.

Feeling better after a shower and some time to calm my nerves, I took a deep breath as I approached the barn with Mr. B jingling along beside me. Stopping, I squatted down and gathered up his long ears. "Okay, buddy." I stared into his droopy brown eyes. "This is it. You gotta stick with me. I may need your moral support."

Mr. B responded by shifting his eyes from side to side, looking a bit perplexed. It would have to do.

"Ready?" I stood up. "Let's go."

With Mr. B protecting my left flank, or at least the lower part of my left leg, I tentatively stepped into the barn, which vibrated with activity and chatter. Locals were everywhere, setting up tables and chairs, hanging twinkling lights, shoving hay bales into a circular pattern. They were so busy, in fact, that my entrance went unnoticed. Thank goodness. That is until Miriam looked up from where she was arranging pumpkins on a table and saw me standing there. She smiled and waved me over. Oh boy, did I feel awkward.

As I made my way to Miriam, Mr. B peeled away from me when he noticed Trudy trotting toward him. Traitor. I was going to have to take my medicine on my own. "Hi," I said when I got to Miriam, concentrating really hard on trying not to blush, which for me is kind of like trying not to get wet when you jump in a lake.

"Good to see you, Sydney. You moved your motorhome."

Did she raise her eyebrows? Quickly looking away, I feigned interest in the table decorations. "Yes, I did. I thought I mentioned that to you. There's no electricity at Cal's right now. Copper theft."

"That's right. Well, it's a lot nicer out here anyway."

"It is that." Fingering the fake fall leaves that Miriam had set around the pumpkins and not wanting to get into what made Noah's ranch so nice, I changed the subject. "How's Ruthie doing?"

"She's all right under the circumstances, poor thing. Naturally she's very worried about Angela."

"I am too."

"I don't think Samuel will allow her to come into harm's way."

"He already has." I frowned.

"I'm sure Patrick and the other deputies are doing all they can to find her."

"I hope so. And I hope it's soon. Otherwise Samuel's going to be long gone to Mexico, and Angela with him." I was annoyed with Miriam's positive attitude about that bastard.

"There's not going to be enough room for the food," a voice said from behind Miriam. It was Odelia, pushing her walker. She was so short I hadn't noticed her approach.

"We don't need these." Odelia reached out and picked up one of the smaller pumpkins by its stem.

"They're fine." Miriam put her hand around the pumpkin Odelia was holding and set it back down. "They look festive."

"There's not going to be enough room for the food," Odelia repeated.

"Yes there is, Odelia. It will be fine." Miriam placed her tall frame between the pumpkins and Odelia, and used me as a diversionary tactic. "You remember Sydney. That was her motorhome that we parked by." At least she hadn't told Odelia about seeing me in the kitchen earlier.

"Of course. Bruised tailbone." Odelia squinted up at me.

No hello, just the same reference she made every time I saw her to the tailbone I bruised at their ranch. In Odelia's mind, I guess I was going to forever be identified by the state of my butt. That's okay. I'd take it over *the harlot sleeping with Noah*, which is the verdict I imagined Odelia announcing if she knew we were having an affair. Although technically, as Solomon's *second* wife, by some folk's standards shriveled old Odelia was right there with me in sinville.

"There you are," Noah said, as he walked up to the table and put his arm around my shoulder.

Odelia narrowed her eyes, looking from one to the other of us. With my conjecture about the state of her own morals on my mind, I ignored her.

"Ladies." Noah nodded at them and turned to me. "I want you to meet my folks." He dropped his arm to his side.

I followed Noah's glance across the room to where his parents were helping hang fairy lights from rafters. Shoot. It was going to be a lot harder to ignore their judgments than Odelia's. Unlike his dad, she hadn't seen my half-naked body in Noah's kitchen.

"We'll catch up with you later." Noah nodded again at the two women.

"Bye." I raised my fingers at them, but made no effort to move until I felt Noah's gentle nudge in the small of my back.

With my heart picking up speed, we crossed the barn. "This is mortifying!" I whispered.

"You're going to be fine," he whispered back. "They don't usually grill my girlfriends over hot coals until they get to know them better."

"What!" I slowed.

"I'm teasing." He smiled at me, his eyes bright, as he grabbed my hand and squeezed it. "Lighten up. They're good people."

Noah's father had just reached the bottom of the ladder when we walked up. His mother was standing to the side with a handful of lights.

"It's looking good." Noah stared up at the rafters, which were heavily wrapped in lights.

"Just a few to go," his father said, and looked over at me, recognition dawning in his eyes.

Tamping down my awkwardness, I filled my brain with self-talk: *Be confident. You can handle this. Breathe.* I smiled at his dad, hoping to pull off casual and relaxed. Sure.

"Dad, Mom, this is Sydney," Noah said, and took the lights from his mother. "Sydney, this is my father Wayne and my mother Anne."

"Nice to meet you." I extended my hand to Anne then to Wayne. Her hands, tanned and spotted from years in the sun, were thin but sturdy, like those of an artist. His hands, equally as tanned and spotted, were large and calloused.

"Noah tells us you're from Los Angeles," Anne said, her voice firm and strong.

"Yes. Well, I was anyway. Now I'm ..." I hesitated, my self-talk fading at the realization I didn't have an answer to the most basic of questions, where do you live? "I guess you could say that I'm between cities right now."

"And you're a writer?"

Casting my eyes at Noah, I wondered how much he'd told them about me. I wasn't sure if my being the subject of discussion was a good thing or a bad thing. "Yes, or I like to think of myself as one. Right now it doesn't pay the bills, so I work as a copy editor."

"You must telecommute, then." Her comment indicated that her scope of knowledge about work in the 21st century extended beyond the confines of a ranch. I was impressed.

"Well, yes." Looking from Anne's serious light brown eyes to Wayne's bright blues ones, it was clear where Noah got his. Although Noah had said his parents wouldn't grill me, it was beginning to feel a bit like an interrogation.

Wayne must have thought so too, because he said, "Are you looking forward to the round dance?"

"Sure. That is, if I can remember the steps."

"Avery's a great cuer. He makes it easy."

"For those of you who know what you're doing. Noah says you do a lot of swing dancing."

"We do. It's great for body and soul."

"I'll bet."

An older man in a plaid shirt and down vest holding a bundle of extension cords walked up. "Say, Noah, where should we hook up the power?"

"Hang on, I'll show you." Noah handed the lights back to his mother. "Best get back at it. Lots to do."

"What would you like me to do?" I asked.

"Follow me. When I'm through with this you can help me finish covering the workbench and fixing it up as a bar."

"There's going to be alcohol?"

"Punch," Anne said.

"With a kick," Wayne added, his eyes sparkling.

"No." Anne jabbed Wayne's arm with her free hand.

"Depends on who's pouring." Wayne smiled.

"Wayne," Anne warned.

"Just be sure to get your punch when *I'm* tending the bowl," he said to me in a stage whisper. "I'll fix you up."

"Okay, that's a deal," I whispered back.

"Nice meeting you," I said to them both as I turned to follow Noah.

Looking back at me as I trailed him and the other man, Noah smiled and winked as if to say, *that wasn't so bad*.

And it wasn't. They *were* good people.

CHAPTER NINE

After I helped in the barn for a while and Noah headed out to get some work done on his ranch, I decided to go back to the motorhome to give Dori a call about the car I saw the night before. Fortunately there was so much to do to get the barn ready for the round dance that my interactions with Miriam, Odelia, Wayne and Anne had been brief. If any of them were curious about the nature of my relationship with Noah, they were going to be left wondering.

When I told Dori about the sedan, she was up for taking a ride with me to investigate. She was between shifts with nothing to do and getting antsier by the day to get back to L.A.

"This is where they turned," I said to Dori as I braked and stared down a gravel road not too far from the turnoff to Noah's ranch. "Do you know who lives down there?"

"My family didn't do a lot of socializing." She looked over at me with a wry expression on her face.

"Oh. That's right. I keep forgetting about that unique upbringing of yours. You seem so normal."

"There is no normal."

"I'd like to think *I'm* normal."

"Think it all you want, but you're not."

"Thanks."

"You're welcome. Take it as a compliment."

Hearing the lightness in Dori's voice made me wonder, not for the first time, how she managed to escape that upbringing of hers with such clarity of vision and thought. She had the ability to kid around a bit, even if sarcasm was her favorite brand of humor. She must have been blessed with one strong will. "Shall we see what's down there?" I took my foot off the brake.

"Sure."

As the little hatchback crunched over the gravel road, we saw nothing but sage and sand for a mile—surprise! But after navigating around a sweeping turn, there before us stood a huge plantation house, with columns, the whole bit. In Southern Utah? Among the red rocks? What?

I turned to look at Dori in disbelief. "You didn't know this was down here?"

"No. Like I said, I didn't get out much. But I know whose it is."

"You do?"

"Sure. It's Genevieve Bailey's."

"Of course." I stopped the car and stared out the front window. "It suits her perfectly. Garish. Gaudy. And totally out of place. Check out those statues and fountains. You'd think we were in Italy. But how do you know for sure it's hers?"

"People in the diner talk. It's been described to me more than once—in detail."

"So, what do you want to do?"

"You're sure this is the road you saw the sedan go down?"

"Yeah."

"Well, according to the gossip, I think Genevieve owns everything for miles around here, but I don't think that includes a sedan–she's not the sedan type–so, I don't know. I guess there's no law against knocking on her door and telling her you think you may have spotted Samuel heading this way."

"Actually, I think there is."

"What?" Dori looked confused.

"A law. Notice the *No Trespassing* signs–everywhere! I'm not sure she appreciates visitors."

"Too bad. We're going anyway. We'll tell her we were concerned for her safety."

"Right. She'll believe that."

As we walked up the steps to her front door, it became obvious that Genevieve's home was of the Monet design–much more impressive from a distance. The paint on the trim around the doors, the windows, and on the columns, was peeling; the porch boards were sinking in some spots and lifted in others; and there were cracks in the stained glass inserts on the double front doors. Trouble in Genevieve-land?

Dori pushed on the doorbell and we stepped back to wait, exchanging glances that said we were both a little surprised at the state of Genevieve's house. When no one answered, Dori tried the bell again. After a few moments, a figure appeared through the stained glass.

"What do you want?" a voice said through the door. It wasn't Genevieve's.

"We need to talk with Genevieve. Is she home?" Dori asked.

"Who are you?"

"Dori, from the diner. And Sydney."

The figure disappeared. "Now what?" I asked. "Do you think she's coming back?"

"We're here. Let's give it a few minutes."

Shifting our weight from foot to foot, we held our arms to our chests to ward off the chilly air. I was just about to suggest to Dori that we give up, when the woman finally returned, still talking at us through the door. "She'll see you, but you need to go around back."

"Nice of her to grant us an audience," I said. "Who does she think she is, the queen?"

"Pretty much." Dori started down the steps.

The back of the house was in no better shape than the front. It looked as if at some point someone tried to start a formal garden, but the boxwood was long dead and the lopsided Neptune atop a massive fountain was in serious risk of taking a nosedive into the Utah desert. Poor guy.

As we started up the back steps, we both turned at the same time when we noticed movement in a patio area off to our right. It was her sons, Floyd and Lloyd, slouched on tattered lawn chairs. Cigarette smoke curled over their heads. Or, at least it looked like cigarette smoke. Who knew with those two?

Looking over when they saw our movement, the first flash across their eyes was alarm, followed quickly by defiance. Lifting their chins in unison, they turned their heads away from us.

"Nice kids, huh?" I said to Dori under my breath.

"Oh, yeah." She fired a look of contempt in their direction. The two of them had made a pastime of torturing Luke, and she had no patience for them.

When we got to the back door, a young harried woman was waiting for us. "Hello," we said, as she held the door open for us and we walked by her.

Stopping in the service porch, we heard the sound of laundry tumbling in a dryer and smelled the sweet floral scent of dryer sheets. Not looking straight at us, the woman said softly, "Sorry you had to come around back. The front door's stuck."

"Stuck?" I asked.

"Yeah. We haven't been able to open it for months. It doesn't matter really, no one comes out here anyway." A look of guilt crossed her face. "I'll take you to her."

"Do you live here?" I asked, curious about Genevieve's whole setup.

"No. I'm here on weekdays."

"What's your name?" Dori asked.

"Maggie."

"You're not from Harmony," Dori said.

"No. I come in from Hurricane."

"Enjoy your job?" I asked. I couldn't imagine how anyone could tolerate working for Genevieve.

"It pays." She dropped her voice and turned away from us. "At least some of the time."

"Yeah. I'll bet she's real magnanimous," I said.

Widening her eyes, a bit of pink flushing her very white cheeks, she ignored my comment. "She's waiting. We better get in there."

We trailed Maggie through the house and into a large formal living room with high ceilings and a large white brick fireplace. Above it hung a life-size painting of Genevieve, reclining on a settee in a low-bodice gown of gauzy gold fabric. Genevieve in the flesh was sitting on an overstuffed couch covered in thick sateen fabric of red and gold. It had lost as much of its luster as she had. Looking from the painting to Genevieve, I estimated she must have sat for it when she was in her twenties.

"My husband loved that painting," Genevieve said when she saw us staring at it. Her tone sounded like she was doing a bad impression of Scarlett O'Hara. I swear, she seriously thought she lived at Tara. Maggie, standing with her head bowed, awaiting her mistress's next command, undoubtedly agreed. Dori and I needed to have a talk with Maggie–alone. There had to be more choices for her than spending her days toiling for the biggest bitch in the county.

"It's, ah, impressive," Dori said. Generous, considering Dori would much rather let Genevieve know what she really thought of her and her sons.

"You can run along now, Maggie, and get back to whatever you were doing," Genevieve said. Again, with the Scarlett O'Hara air. Brother!

After Maggie left the room, Genevieve had still not offered to have us sit down. Just as well. We would probably have kicked up a cloud of dust from the stale-smelling cushions.

"What can I do for you?" She crossed her legs and stretched her arm along the back of the couch. She directed her question to Dori, not having acknowledged I was even in the room. She was not the type to forget about the run-ins I had with her over her precious babies, or about my association with Noah. Just as well. It was making my skin crawl to be breathing the same stuffy air with her anyway.

"Sydney noticed a sedan driving down your road last night." Dori looked over at me. Genevieve followed her glance and narrowed her eyes at me, like I'd done something wrong. "She thinks it may have been the one we spotted Samuel Vaullie in last week in St. George. He kidnapped his daughter, Angela, you know, and is on the run because of his connection to the deaths of two girls and babies from their cult."

"If it's his daughter, how can that be kidnapping?" Genevieve said, with zero empathy in her voice. *That* was what she chose to focus on with all Samuel had done?

"It's kidnapping." Dori worked hard to keep her voice even, but was already losing patience with Genevieve.

"Look, he's a criminal," I spoke up, "and he's got Angela, and he's endangering her life. We think he's still around the area somewhere and I think I saw him drive down your road. Did you see or hear any cars last night?"

"No." She sneered at me. "He'd have no reason to be on my road. There's nothing on it but my property. You must have been seeing things."

"I was not seeing things. It was Samuel." I was not actually sure it was, but she'd pushed me and I wanted to make her wrong.

"Anyway," Dori said, stepping in before it devolved into a shouting match, as usually happened between Genevieve and myself. "If you do notice any unfamiliar cars on your road or if you think that you see Samuel, would you please let Deputy Crane know."

"Oh, like that would help. Crane's worthless." She uncrossed her legs. "If that's all you wanted, I need to get back to what I was doing."

"Thanks," I said in a sarcastic tone.

Genevieve rolled her eyes at me, bent over, and grabbed a magazine from the side table, then sat up straight and began thumbing through it. Now there was something really important to fill her afternoon.

Dori stared at Genevieve's stiff dyed-blonde hair. "Thanks," she echoed in the same tone I had used.

Stepping into the hallway off the living room, we saw the backs of Floyd and Lloyd hurrying away from us at a much faster pace than we had ever seen them move. My radar kicked into gear. "They must have been spying on us."

"Guys!" Dori called after them as they started through the back door. "Wait up a minute."

Pretending they didn't hear us, they kept moving down the steps and around the far side of the house toward the garage. Dori jogged after them. I trailed after her.

"Wait!" she said, as she closed in on them when they got to their car, which was parked in front of the garage. Moving quickly, she blocked one of the twins before he could open the driver's side door. "Lloyd, hang on." I was impressed she could tell them apart. They were Floyd/Lloyd to me.

Looking right and left like he was checking for an escape route, he finally acknowledged Dori. "What do you want?"

"You were listening at the door when we talked with your mother, and now you're in a big hurry to get out of here. Do you know something about Samuel?"

He crossed his arms and stared past her over the top of the car at his brother. "I don't know what you're talking about. Who's Samuel?"

"Don't play dumb." Dori looked from Lloyd to Floyd. "You know who Samuel is. Did you see him last night?"

"We weren't even here." Floyd spoke up from his side of the car.

"Yeah. We weren't here. Now get out of our way." Lloyd reached around Dori for the door handle.

She shifted to block him and stared him down then his brother. "Look, you two. Samuel is a murderer who kidnapped his own daughter and we need to find him before something happens to her."

"He didn't murder nobody," Floyd spit out.

"Shut up! Don't say nothing to these bitches," his brother warned.

"Why would you come to Samuel's defense?" I walked around the car and stepped within inches of Floyd. "Especially when a minute ago you acted like you didn't know who he was?"

"You know something." Dori tapped Lloyd's chest with her finger. "And you need to tell us now."

"We don't need to do nothin'." Lloyd slapped Dori's finger aside. "Get out of here." Shoving his way past Dori, he yanked so hard on the door that she was forced to step out of the way or be hit by it.

Following his brother's lead, Floyd tugged on his door handle and quickly slid into the car. I stepped back from it just in time to have Lloyd jerk it to a start and tear down the drive, spitting gravel.

"They definitely know something," Dori said as we watched the car disappear.

"I'll say. What was with Floyd defending Samuel?"

"I don't know. That was really odd."

"Are they related to him? You all seem to be cousins."

"No." Dori frowned at me. "There are a few more branches on the Harmony family tree than that."

I smiled at her choice of words. "It's still highly suspicious. Should we tell Patrick?"

"Probably." Dori tapped her forefinger on her lips. "But I don't know. If there's a chance the Bailey boys know something about Samuel, we may be better off not setting off any more alarms. Let's give it a little time. See if they either develop consciences and decide to say something, or slip up and drop a clue about what they know."

"Okay. But between our expedition to the mountains on Sunday and this latest scheme, we seem to be working Patrick out of a job."

"Nah." Dori tightened her sweater around her and stared at the red mesa far off in the distance then at me. "I just have a lot more faith in *you* than *him*."

"Really?" I wrinkled my brow. "How am I supposed to live up to that?"

"You're strong, smart and stubborn. You'll live up to it."

"No. That's you, Dori."

"It's you, Syd." She slid her hand under my arm. "You'd know it if you didn't question every damn thing you do."

"Thanks. Nothing like a backhanded compliment to raise the confidence level."

"You're welcome." She propelled us forward. "Now, let's go. I'm freezing."

CHAPTER TEN

Glancing down at my lace-trimmed purple paisley skirt, I was in disbelief. It hung well above my knees and the crinoline petticoat make it pouf out like a birthday girl's party dress. How had Dori talked me into this one? "Everyone wears them," she said. "It's fun." Not! I tugged on the hem of the lace pettipants that came with the round dance uniform. When she showed those little numbers to me, I laughed out loud. She told me I had to wear them unless I wanted God and everybody to discover whether I was a thong underwear or granny-panty girl. Couldn't let that happen.

I had picked up the borrowed outfit from Dori earlier in the day, which was the only time I left the motorhome since our trip to Genevieve's the day before. I had gotten behind on my copy editing and dedicated all of Friday night and Saturday to catching up. I couldn't afford to have my boss Collette terminate our arrangement.

But, it was round dance time! Woo hoo! Grabbing my long coat, I pressed it around my skirt and buttoned up, wondering if I could get away with leaving it on for the night.

After patting Alice on the head and scratching Mr. B behind the ears, I headed out the door. Following the sound of laughter and music to the barn, a rush of anticipation quickened my steps. Pettipants aside, I was genuinely excited to be right there, right then. Crazy. This is Harmony, Utah, I reminded myself. How could you possibly be excited about anything here? And, then I caught the unmistakable profile of Noah in his cowboy hat just inside the door. There *was* that.

"Hey there, let me take your coat," he said as I walked in.

"Um ..." I dug my hands deeper into my pockets. "I'm pretty cold."

"We've got heaters, and when the dancing starts, you'll warm right up."

Looking at the clusters of people spread throughout the barn, there was not one wearing a coat. The women were all dressed like me, the only variation being the color and pattern of the fabric and the length of the skirts. Some of their lace hems reached mid-calf. Why hadn't Dori come up with one of those for me? I began to undo my buttons, but didn't make eye contact with Noah as I did so.

When I finally looked at him as I handed him my coat, he was grinning. The dork! "What!"

"It's not that brown dress you wore to buffalo steak night at Dusty's, but I like it."

"Dori made me." I scowled at him.

"And, I'm glad she did." He smiled down at my bare legs.

"And, I'm still cold!" Goose bumps peppered those legs he found so interesting.

"Then, let's warm you up." Putting his arm around my waist, he walked me across the room to the long workbench bar, which was flanked by two tall propane heaters. His father was manning a large punchbowl and a very large cooler.

"Sydney! Glad you made it. You look real pretty tonight," Wayne said as we walked up.

"Thank you. Not a fashion design you come across much in Los Angles." I ran my hands down the skirt, trying to control the flare of the petticoat.

"You've been traveling in the wrong circles, young lady." He stirred the punch with a ladle. "There are so many round and square dance clubs in your old neck of the woods, you could go to ten different dances a night."

"Really?"

"Why sure." He picked up a plastic cup, his eyes sparkling. "You ready to wet your whistle?"

"Okay."

Reaching behind the cooler, he pulled out a tall flask and held it up to me. "Shall I add some hooch? Kick her up a notch?"

I looked over at Noah to see his reaction. "Are you having some?"

"Yeah. But I'm taking mine hoochless. You know how rowdy Harmony folks can get."

"At a round dance?"

"No. But, it's my barn. I best keep a clear head."

"I've never seen you without one, come to think of it. Do you ever let loose?"

"Nah," Wayne spoke for Noah. "He's too earnest, like his mother. But there's no reason for *you* to miss out on the fun." He tipped the flask toward the cup.

"Why not? But, not too much, please."

"That a girl." Wayne poured in plenty and topped it off with the punch.

"Thanks." I raised my cup and took a sip. It was very sweet, which masked the alcohol, a dangerous combination. I wasn't going back for seconds.

After Wayne poured a cup for Noah, we moved away from the table. "Shall I call you Ernest?" I said.

"Mr. Thompson will do just fine."

"Okay then, Mr. Thompson, when does the dancing start?" I noticed people honed in on the buffet tables. "They seem a lot more interested in eating than dancing." I nodded toward them.

"They'll be ready when Avery starts things up. Are *you* ready?"

"I guess. How does the whole partner thing work?" I wasn't quite clear on whether the evening was a date for the two of us. I had been wondering if he was going to stick with me all night, or if I was going to have to count on V.A. to help fill my dance card.

"The couples who are serious about it, the ones who compete, and most married folks don't change partners, but everyone else mixes it up."

"You mean there are competitions? Like the round dance Olympics?"

"If you can win a prize for eating the most hot dogs in a minute, why not one for round dancing?"

"I guess I get that." I laughed. Then my junior high school brain crept into my consciousness. "Who are you mixing it up with this evening? I see that Genevieve is here." I glanced across the room at her. She was wearing the same basic outfit as the rest of us, only it was fire engine red and her blouse was so low cut there was only an inch or two between the bottom of her cleavage and the top of her wide cloth belt.

Jeez! I scolded myself. Why did I bring *that* up? It had to have been the meeting with Genevieve the previous day. And the one before that. And the one before that.

"Oh, there's Dori," I said before Noah could answer, hoping to cover my descent into puberty. "I'm going to go say hi to her."

Wrapping his hand around my arm before I could step away, Noah leaned into my ear, pressing the folds of my skirt to my thigh. "There's only one woman in this room I plan on mixing it up with tonight, but that will be after the lights are out and everyone's gone home."

Feeling his hot breath on my neck, I swallowed and whispered, "Okay. I'm glad we cleared that up."

After giving my neck a short kiss that left a long trail of chills, Noah put his finger to the brim of his hat, cast me a smoky stare and walked away.

Oh my goodness, the guy was so much more intoxicating than whatever Wayne put in my cup. Noticing a garbage can a few feet away and turning to make sure Wayne wasn't watching, I walked over and dropped my cup into it. Noah wasn't the only one who wanted to keep a clear head for what was coming later in the evening.

When I walked up to Dori, she was refilling a tray of mashed potatoes at the buffet table. She had told me that she and Luke were on tap to help Dusty out, as he was the official round dance caterer. Patrick was there in uniform, mounding his plate with one of everything. For a skinny man, he sure could eat a lot.

"Dori, Sydney," Patrick acknowledged us.

"Hi," we both answered.

"Any word on Samuel?" Dori asked. We still hadn't told him about the sedan I had seen, or her suspicion that Samuel was hiding out in the mountains.

"No. And, we had another copper theft last night."

"Oh, no," I said. "In Harmony?"

"Yep. The phone lines behind V.A.'s."

"She's not going to be happy about that," Dori said. "V.A.'s likely to track the thieves down herself, and string them up on a fence."

Not unlike someone else I know, I thought, still unconvinced that Dori and I should be tackling the investigation of Samuel on our own.

"The good news is the office in St. George thinks they may have a solid lead on the gang that's responsible for a lot of the recent thefts."

"Cal will be glad to hear about that," I said.

"What's that you say?" It was Cal, who had just walked up with his girlfriend Lou. Somehow the term *girlfriend* didn't quite fit her. Cattlewoman, horsewoman, scary woman, but girlfriend, not so much.

"Our office in St. George is closing in on the gang they believe has been stealing the copper in the county," Patrick said to Cal.

"Good to hear. Any word on when they might be going after their sorry asses?"

"No. But I'm guessing it won't be long. The crooks are getting more brazen by the day. I was just telling them that they stripped the telephone lines behind V.A.'s last night."

Cal sucked in his breath between his teeth. "Man, I bet she's madder than a wet hornet. Too bad she didn't hear nothin'."

"That would've been helpful, but they usually strike in the middle of the night."

"Like vampires," I said.

"Speakin' a this," Cal turned his attention to me, "the electrical panel is up and runnin' if you wanna move your motorhome ... Ouch!" He stopped in mid-sentence, looked down at his shin then over at Lou, a puzzled expression on his face. "What'd you do that for, Honeybunch?"

She didn't answer; just bored her eyes into his instead.

With Cal standing there, still confused, I decided I better intervene before Lou decided to take out his other shin. "It's working out fine having the motorhome here. Noah ..."

"I'll bet it is," Lou cut me off and crossed her arms.

Okay? There I was, trying to cover up for her maiming her boyfriend and Lou shoots insinuations at me? She and Genevieve ought to pair up–tag-team sniping. I willed myself to take the high road. "Yes, like Cal, Noah is a generous man and I appreciate the help."

"I suppose things are real different in California, because the women from around here, the ones I associate with, don't need to call on the generosity of gullible men. We do just fine on our own."

I glanced at Patrick and Cal, who had gone completely still and who were looking more than a little stunned, then back at Lou's pinched face. The low road it was! "Nice way to treat Cal. Accusing him of being gullible!" I stared her down, trying hard to keep my voice from trembling. "If those women you associate with have a disposition half as nasty as yours, I bet they have no trouble remaining on their own. What man would ever want them? And if Cal weren't such an even-tempered guy, he probably would've left you years ago!"

"Wouldn't you just like that, to have him free to get your claws deeper into him." Lou didn't seem rattled at all. She just held her position, like she was cemented to the floor.

Losing air and with the blood whooshing in my ears, I also just stood there. Then I heard Noah ask from behind me, "So, what all you got there, Dori?"

She waved a large serving spoon like it was a flag. "The mashed potatoes are nice and hot. And we have some tasty looking ribs and cornbread."

"Great. We'll grab some plates and help ourselves." Nudging me to the table, Noah reached around me, picked up two thick paper plates and handed one to me.

As Cal also started to pick up a plate, Lou reached out and grabbed him by the arm. "We're not eating right now," she said in a commanding tone.

"We're not?"

"No."

"But I'm hungry, Honeybunch."

"I told the Johnsons we'd eat with them."

"But they're always late." Cal stood his ground.

"Let's get a beer, and you can grab some chips off the other table." She tugged on him. "Come along, now."

Staring longingly at the ribs, he turned to leave.

Leaning toward him, I said softly, "Thanks for the offer Cal. I do appreciate your kindnesses to me." Looking over my shoulder, I stared directly at Lou, and I stuck my tongue out at her. I'm not proud of it. But it felt *so good*.

Before Cal walked away, he whispered under his breath. "'Tweren't nothin'."

When I turned back to the table, Dori was smiling. "Did you stick your tongue out at her?"

"Yes." I started to laugh. I suppressed it, though, when Noah looked over at me, not smiling. "What? You don't think she deserved that with the way she was talking to me?"

"I didn't hear what she was saying. I just noticed your body language."

"Oh, yeah? And what did that tell you?"

"You were pretty animated."

"Rightfully so. She thinks you're gullible and that I manipulated you into helping me. And you!" I pointed the tongs from the tray of ribs at Dori. "Why didn't you speak up?"

"You were doing more than fine on your own." Dori smiled again.

"Anyway, I just don't get why he's with that woman. Cal's a really good guy and he's smarter than people think."

"Maybe he's not thinking with his brain," Dori said.

It took me a couple tics to get her meaning, and I stared across the room to where Cal and Lou were holding beers and talking to Wayne. "Ew." I set the tongs back down on the tray.

"Can I serve you some salad?" Dori said to Noah when she saw him looking less than pleased with the direction we had taken the conversation.

"Can you eat with us?" I asked Dori, piggybacking on her diversionary tactic. We could save the rest of the conversation about Cal and Lou for when we were out of earshot of Noah. No doubt he was far too perfect to indulge in anything he considered gossip.

"Sure. Just let me get Luke to take my place. He's been talking Patrick's ear off for the last few minutes, undoubtedly with all kinds of thoughts on their trip to the Bliss Mine tomorrow.

"Where should we eat?" I asked Noah, who now had a full plate.

"How about with V.A.?" He pointed his chin at a picnic bench, where V.A. was engaged in conversation with a large man and a young woman who could have been his daughter. I couldn't help but notice it was at the opposite end of the barn from where Cal and Lou were still standing.

"Good choice," I said. "You wanna meet us there, Dori?"

"Sure. See you in a few."

The crowd finally ebbed away from the buffet tables. The music started up. Avery took the microphone, and a rainbow of skirts and western shirts circled the dance floor like a carousel on a lazy Sunday afternoon. The round dancing was quite graceful, impressive considering many of the dancers' alter egos spent their days slinging hay, manure, or in Dusty's case, hash. I mention Dusty, because he was a popular dance partner, so light on his boots that he had the ladies standing in line for their turn. I had a turn while Noah danced with Lou. She finagled that when I had my back turned. I would have danced with Cal, but I was hesitant to provide the crowd with a floorshow of Lou tossing me around by my hair.

Fire-engine-red Genevieve also had her dance with Noah. Of course. It irritated the hell out of me, but I wasn't about to let it show. I also didn't have to watch. I asked Dori if she wanted to take a breather outside.

"She's nothing to him, you know," Dori said when we stepped through the barn door into the star-filled night.

I waved her off. "You think I care about that?"

"Yeah."

"No." When Dori rolled her eyes at me, I said, "Okay, I care a little. Why does he have to be so damn nice to that low-life? And Lou, too? The guy's terminally agreeable."

"Ha!" Dori laughed. "That's the first time I've heard that one."

"It's true. It's annoying."

"You're annoyed because he's a decent guy?"

"Well, when you put it that way." I laughed too.

"Brr. It's too cold out here." Dori hugged her arms to her chest and stamped her feet. "We should've grabbed our coats."

"That's okay, we can head back in." I started to walk back through the door when the sound of voices in the distance stopped me. Dori heard it too. "Is that Luke?" I squinted at three figures standing by Dusty's pickup truck, which was parked next to my motorhome.

"Yeah, it is. And that's the Bailey boys with him!" Dori hurried toward them. I followed on her heels.

When we reached them, Luke was bent over several upturned pans and the remnants of mashed potatoes and cornbread. "What's going on?" Dori demanded, looking from one to the other of the twins.

"Your brother's a retard, that's what," one of them said to her.

Dori slapped him fast and hard. His hand shot to his cheek.

"Hey!" The other brother stuck his chest out and moved toward us. "You wanna fight, bitch. We'll fight you!"

"Wait!" I slid my body between them and Dori. "Slow down! You don't want to do this." I held up both palms. "Deputy Crane is right inside and would be happy to haul you off to jail again."

"She started it! Let him haul *her* off to jail!"

"*You* started it," I said. "Those pans didn't land on the ground by themselves. You've been harassing Luke and I'm guessing you're in violation of your sentence by being out here tonight."

"I'm gonna get her for this!" The one who Dori struck dropped his hand and started to move toward us.

"No!" I shouted. "You're not doing this!"

Dori moved in beside me. I could feel the anger radiating from her. Not good.

"Let's just calm down. You're clearly in the wrong here, boys. Don't make it worse for yourselves. Leave now and we won't call Deputy Crane out here. If he hauls you in, the judge is going to go a whole lot harder on you than the last time. Think about it." I stared at each of them, holding my breath.

They looked from one to the other of us with their jaws clenched and hatred in their eyes. "Let's go," the one who Dori hit said, finally backing down and jerking his head toward the pasture beyond the pickup truck, where people had parked for the dance. "But this isn't over!" he snarled at us, as he turned and led his brother into the dark.

Dori walked over to Luke, and I took a step in the direction the boys had gone to make sure they left the ranch. Just about the time I lost sight of their backs, I noticed a still figure standing next to a car and looking my direction. It was far too dark to discern the face or the make of the car, but the tingling in my spine said it had to be Samuel Vaullie. No! Why?

After we picked up the pans and helped Luke put them into Dusty's truck, we walked back to rejoin the dance, although our enthusiasm for the event had diminished considerably. Dori reassured Luke that they weren't going to have to put up with the Bailey boys for much longer, because she planned to move back to L.A. very soon. That seemed to help. When he walked into the barn Luke headed straight for Patrick, the thought of the Bailey boys lost to his excitement about his upcoming trip to the Bliss Mine. Patrick was a patient man.

Placing my hand on Dori's forearm, I stopped her before we moved closer to the group of people standing nearby. "Samuel was out there," I whispered loud enough for her to hear over the music.

"No!" Several heads turned in our direction.

Grabbing her arm, I leaned into her ear. "I can't be certain because there's hardly any light out there, but I've seen him enough to make out his big ugly head and stubby legs. It had to be him. But why? Why would he risk showing up here? And why is he watching us?"

"God only knows. He's a wicked mean man, full of spite. There's any number of things he could be planning."

"Great." I shivered, and not from the cold. "And you want to go after him?"

"We need to find out where he's hiding Angela. When we do, we'll let Patrick know. We won't go after him by ourselves."

"You promise?" I moved to where I was facing her. "Because we can't do her or anyone any good if we end up captive just like her."

"I promise."

"No risky business?"

"No risky business."

"Good." I hoped I could count on her word.

She glanced over at the buffet table. "It looks like there are a few things that still need to be cleaned up. I better get over there."

"Are you going to say anything to Patrick about the Bailey boys?" I walked with her over to the table.

"Probably. But it won't do any good. They'll never change."

"How about Genevieve? Are you going to tell her?" I looked for her on the dance floor. She was hard to miss. Clinging to an uncomfortable rancher, she was making up her own dance steps, three sheets to the wind, probably having guzzled more than her fair share of Wayne's hooch.

"She'd just blame me."

"True."

"I'm so glad Luke and I are getting out of here." Dori started collecting serving utensils from the buffet table and putting them in a box she pulled out from underneath it. "If we don't hear from Malachi soon, I'm going to see if Harry can find me another place. When I get back, I'll just stay away from the shelter for awhile."

"Sounds kinda chancy."

"And living here isn't?"

CHAPTER ELEVEN

"Dori! Wait up! I'm stuck again!" I dug my poles into the ground beneath the thick layer of fresh snow and tried to lift my foot, but it wasn't going anywhere. Dori and I had been pounding through the Pine Valley Mountains for over two hours and my legs were so tired they were trembling.

"How much longer?" I said when Dori trudged back to me and tamped down the area around my feet with her snowshoes so we could continue on our forced march. "My bod has had it."

"I just want to check around that bend in the road ahead. I remember seeing cabins when I was up here hiking last summer."

"We've already passed by several places and haven't run into a soul. That road, if you can call it that, hasn't even been plowed and there are no tire tracks going through it."

"It's the only part of this area we haven't explored. Let's not give up now."

"Okay, fine, but I'm going to be sore for weeks." Duckwalking like Dori taught me, I followed her up the incline and onto the road, thinking it might have been one of the most ridiculous things I'd ever done. We didn't even have a plan. What if we did stumble across Samuel and the other men? We sure couldn't beat them in a footrace if they spotted us, and my car was so far back I didn't even want to think about it.

With the walking easier on the flat road, we picked up our pace. As we rounded the curve, we saw a curl of smoke rising from a small weather-beaten cabin. Halting, Dori waited for me to catch up.

"Now what?" I asked.

"Step into the trees and hide yourself." She pointed to the stand of spruce that lined the road. "I'll check it out."

"But they'll see you."

"I'll stick to the shadow of the mountain and circle around the back of the cabin."

"If you see anything that looks suspicious, come right back, okay? Don't get too close."

"Sure." She started up the far side of the road.

Hugging my arms to my chest, I twisted my body from side to side, trying to stay warm while I waited. Why on earth had I given up a long lazy morning between cozy flannel sheets with Noah for this! I looked overhead at the snow bomb resting precariously on the limb directly above my head and took a giant step back. I must be out of my mind! Noah hadn't made it easy to leave at all, with his body feeling like hard muscle wrapped in warm velvet. And yet, here I was.

When I told Noah about my plan for the day, I made no mention of searching for Angela, because he would have insisted I tell Patrick our real objective. And the longer I stood there wondering what the heck happened to Dori, the more right I thought Noah would have been. Just as I was about to come out from behind my tree to check on Dori, I heard her softly calling my name.

"Over here," I said, stepping onto the road.

Dori was stopped in the middle of it, waving me toward her.

When I reached her, she said, "You're not going to believe this."

"Okay."

"The old guy who lives in that cabin ... he's ... well, you have to see for yourself." She tromped off at a much faster pace than I could manage. What had she gotten us into now?

Leaving my snowshoes on the porch and mimicking Dori, who stomped her feet to rid herself of the last traces of snow, I followed her through the portal. It was so low I barely cleared it. Stepping into the room, I stopped for a few seconds to let my eyes adjust to the dim light.

When it came into focus, there before me was a room built of logs, aged coffee brown. A fireplace filled almost an entire wall and crackled with the primordial scent of burning pine and pitch. Hanging from nails tacked into every one of those logs were stone and crystal pendants of every shape, color, and size. The light glinting off them moved like a family of rainbow-hued ghosts that had taken up permanent residence. Above our heads, suspended from large beams, were dozens of fork-shaped tree branches.

As I dropped my eyes back to the room, they lighted on an ancient man sitting on a willow rocker, which creaked to the rhythm of his slow movements back and forth, back and forth.

"Sydney, this is Emmet." Dori walked me over to stand in front of him.

"Hello," I said, searching for his eyes under a faded baseball cap he had pulled down to wiry brows that grew long and in every direction.

"Sydney," he said with the last vestiges of a New England accent. "Sit." He nodded to a small bench that was tucked under a hand-hewn rectangular table.

Dori and I pulled the bench out and angled it so we were directly across from him and only a few feet away.

"Emmet's a diviner," Dori said.

"What?" I asked.

"A water diviner. He finds water with those divining rods." She cast her eyes at the branches above us.

"Oh, I saw something about that on TV. You're called dowsers too, and water witches, right?" I followed her glance.

"A witch I'm not," Emmet said.

Oops. "Sorry." I dropped my eyes back down. I had insulted the host, and he seemed none too happy. Or was that the way he always looked? It was hard to tell under the cap. He fascinated me, nonetheless. It's not every day you come across someone who thinks he can *divine* the source of water. "How does it work?" I asked.

A bit of light came into his faded gray eyes as he began to speak. "Everything's made of the same basic matter." He pointed his chin in an almost indistinguishable movement at a large turquoise stone resting on the small log end table next to him. "Rocks. Trees. Water. You. Me. That matter's infused with an all-knowing spirit. Still the mind. Listen." He closed his eyes. "Listen to the earth, the plants, animals, and the voice that speaks when we quiet our own, and all knowledge is ours." His eyes flashed open and he bore them into mine. "A gift. For the greater good, or our annihilation. Our choice."

Okeydoke. Time to go. He was taking the *divine* part way too seriously. Looking over at Dori, it seemed Emmet's flight into fantasyland hadn't fazed her at all. I, on the other hand, wanted out of there. If we hurried I might be able to talk Noah back into those flannel sheets before lunch.

Tilting her head up to look at the branches above us, Dori asked, "Why do you have so many?"

"Picked 'em up from all over when I was an earth traveler. Now my spirit does all the traveling." His fingers tapped gently against the arms of the rocker in a steady rhythm.

"Don't get much call for dowsing anymore?" Dori asked, not noticing I had moved to the edge of the bench, anxious to leave.

"Nah. Folk's misplaced faith in machinery–you can't fight it. Don't want to."

"And the stones? What are all of these for?" She stood up, stepped over to the closest wall and fingered a pendant of pink quartz hanging at eye level.

"Energy fields. And truth. You looking for it; they'll lead you there." He rocked slowly forward, put his weight on his hands and slowly stood up. Picking up a crudely carved cane that was leaning against the table, he tapped his way over to Dori and stood shoulder to shoulder with her in front of the log wall.

Oh, boy, I thought. We're never going to get out of here.

"How'd you get into all this?" Dori asked.

"I didn't. It came to me by way of my parents and their parents before them, going back to the beginning."

"Do you think they could help us find the girl we're looking for?"

What! I stared at the back of Dori's head. What had come over her? I hadn't known her that long, but she seemed far too practical to be a voodoo worshipper.

"Let me see what I can pick up." Emmet slowly inched along the wall, touching the pendants as he went. Reaching out, he removed a bright blue stone with flecks of gold and sea green that dangled from a leather string. Encasing it in his hand, he closed his eyes and held onto it for several seconds. "Yes, this is it." He stepped over to the table and sat down on the bench.

We pulled the bench where we had been sitting up to the table opposite him.

"Hold this, close your eyes and calm your breath." He handed the stone to Dori.

Dori held it in her fist, which rested on the table, and took several deep breaths.

"That's fine, now." He opened his palm for her to hand the pendant back to him and suspended it over the top of the table. Looking over at me, he said. "You need to remove your negative energy, or this won't work."

I flushed like I'd been caught cheating on an exam. "You want me to leave?"

"Yes. You can wait in the bedroom." He motioned to the door next to the wall that held the stove and sink. "And while you're in there, focus your mind on a pleasant memory, what you're having for supper, anything that doesn't get your dander up. And keep it off us."

"Okay." Feeling like a punished schoolgirl, I swung my legs from under the table and padded across the wood floor and into his bedroom.

How the hell was I going to keep my mind off them and the wacky scene I just left?

"Take some deep breaths. It'll help." Emmet called to me through the door in a voice strong and clear for someone I estimated to be about ninety.

The hairs on the back of my neck pricked up. Did he just read my mind? No. Obeying his command, I took three deep breaths and looked for a place to sit while I waited. There was a stool far too short for my long legs under the window that I contemplated using, but I wasn't sure I could get up from it without help. I opted to pace the room instead.

Trying to obey orders, I decided to make mental lists as a way to distract my mind. I started with what I needed to get done for my editing work, moved onto the article I was doing about polygamy, and made a list of what I needed to pick up at the grocery store. That took all of about three minutes. Now what?

Noticing a framed black and white photo on the table next to the bed, I picked it up. It was of a woman, with her hair curled in a style popular in the 1940s. Emmet's wife? Next to it was a small book, with its title, *The Voice of Silence,* embossed in gold on a faded and worn dark blue cover. I sat down on the edge of the bed, fanned through it, and started reading paragraphs here and there. "Have patience, Candidate, as one who fears no failure, courts no success. Fix thy Soul's gaze upon the star whose ray thou ..."

"We're done." Dori opened the door and stuck her head around it.

"Good." I set the book back in its place, popped up and followed her to the fireplace.

Emmet was returning the pendant to its spot on the wall. Moving along it once again, he picked out a stone that was deep-ocean blue, a white one, and one that was a coral pink with uneven black spots. He walked over to us, holding them with the hand not occupied by the cane.

"Lapis lazuli." He held the blue one out to Dori. "Wear this."

She took it and slid it over her head.

"Lapis has been here since the beginning of time. It'll lead you to your higher truth and send any negative energy that attempts to penetrate your life back to its source."

"Thank you." Dori fingered the stone.

"And this is moonstone." He held it out to her. "Wear this when you're with those women you help. It's the stone of destiny. It'll bring you and them harmony, health, and protection."

She took it and layered it over the lapis pendant.

"And this, my dear, is for you." He held out the pink and black stone. "It's rhodonite and will help calm your impatience and ground your negative energy. It'll also help your love arise and clarify your passion."

I'm not that negative, I wanted to say, but I took the stone and draped it over my head.

A twinkle came into his eyes when he caught my look. "Just hold on to the stone, Sydney, and think lovely thoughts."

Think lovely thoughts? So now he's quoting *Peter Pan*? How'd he know that was my favorite Disney movie? Maybe he *was* clairvoyant. Nah. But he was a likeable character. One to file away for that novel I was going to write. Someday. Maybe.

"We need to go," Dori said, reaching out her hands and wrapping them over his, which were resting on the cane. "Thank you for your time and your help."

"Yes, thank you," I said, gently resting my hand on his shoulder.

He nodded.

"I appreciate your agreeing to keep an eye out for Samuel and Angela," Dori said.

"I don't have a phone, you know."

"Yes. You mentioned that. That's okay. I'm going to leave you my number anyway, in case the cousin you told me about stops by and you want to reach me." She rummaged in the small backpack she brought along, pulled out a scrap piece of paper and pen and wrote her contact information. "If we haven't found Angela in the next few days, we'll head back up here, maybe try a different area. We'll pop in then."

We will? I frowned at Dori. What *we?* There was no way she was going to get me back in snowshoes. Ever.

"What do you do in case of an emergency? None of your neighbors seem to be around." I was curious about how he managed without a phone, and without a car. I hadn't noticed one anywhere near the cabin.

"I don't have emergencies." He tugged on the brim of his cap.

Must be nice. But, he did have to eat. "What about food? How do you get to the store?"

"I keep a stocked pantry. My cousin takes me into Leeds every once in a while."

I started to say something about it being a lonely life, then I caught the glint of the crystals shining from every corner of the firelit room. It had to feel as if he were living in the center of a prism. I looked over at Emmet to find he had been watching me. The serenity in his look conveyed that he was perfectly content with his lot. Not a bad way to spend the last of his years. I nodded at him.

"We sure came up empty-handed on this adventure." I turned my eyes from the road to look over at Dori. We were a little less than halfway back to Harmony and she'd been very quiet. I wondered if it was because she knew I was expecting her to tell me the story of her polygamist childhood as promised, but changed her mind. Several times on the way up I wanted to initiate the discussion, but was sensitive to the pain that revisiting her past may cause her.

"No, we didn't." Dori straightened in her seat. "We just need to expand our search area."

"Oh, good. You want me to walk even farther on those things." I gestured with my thumb to the snowshoes piled on the backseat. "Thanks, anyway."

"You had fun."

"Oh, is that what you call it?" I rubbed one hand down my sore thigh muscle. "I just don't see how you expect to find Angela in all this." I looked out at the high desert stretched out before us. "They could be anywhere."

"But they're not. I know they're back there in the Pine Valley Mountains."

"Is that what you and Emmet *divined*?" It came out sarcastic.

"He just confirmed what I already felt in my gut." Her own tone was defensive.

"So, how did the whole pendulum thing work?" I softened my voice, not wanting to risk alienating Dori. That past she kept to herself must have made it difficult for her to build trust. I didn't want to land on the other side of the walls she put up to protect herself and Luke.

"He held the pendulum over the table and we asked it questions. It goes one direction for yes and the other for no." She tucked her legs up under her and shifted to face me.

"You really think that works? It kinda puzzles me that you'd buy into that stuff, especially as a runaway from a nutso pseudo-spiritual cult." I smiled to let her know there was no judgment in my statement.

"There's no true spirituality in those cults—at all. They're just a cover for abuse, pedophilia, and illegal businesses. Emmet's beliefs are nothing like that. They're a lot more like the Native practices you find here in the Southwest. I do believe we're spiritually connected to other people, animals, and nature. Don't you?"

I visualized Mr. Bumbles greeting me at the motorhome door and Alice stretched out on my bed. "Yeah, I suppose I do."

"And if it wasn't for inner guidance, you would've never left L.A. or landed here."

"I'm here because I got lost."

"You just keep telling yourself that." Her dark eyes shone.

With her mood lightening, I decided to open the discussion about her life. "Hey, Dori, if you're up to it, I'd like to ask you a few questions about your childhood and polygamy for the article, like we discussed. But you don't have to, you know, if it makes you too uncomfortable."

"No." She sighed. "I told you I'd do it, and I should. People need to know how bad it is."

As Dori began to spool out the threads of her childhood, my stomach churned with the depravity she revealed. She was the daughter of her father's third wife; a woman cowed by abuse from both her husband and his other wives. From a very young age, Dori said she knew she was never going to succumb like her mother. It landed her a lot of beatings over the years, but worked to hold off the pedophiles until she was fifteen. When her father started talking about making her the second wife of her twenty-five-year-old cousin, she decided she was leaving and she was taking Luke, her youngest brother, with her. She knew that with his special needs, they'd end up kicking him out anyway, and he'd never survive on the streets.

The first two times Dori and Luke tried to escape their family dragged them back. Finally, she created such a scene they decided she wasn't worth it. They kicked her out and let her take Luke with her. It was Dusty's sister, Marilyn, who took them in. She had formed an organization to help refugees from polygamy, much like the one Dori now belonged to. They lived with Marilyn for the first few years, and she helped them both with their schooling and adjusting to life on the outside.

Marilyn got so frustrated with the lack of support in fighting the abuses of polygamy, however, that she folded her organization and left the state. By that time Dori had been working for Dusty for quite a while and she and Luke had moved to the apartment above the garage.

"Wow," I said, shaking my head when she finished speaking. "You were one brave young woman."

"I'm not sure it was so much bravery as orneriness." She brushed off the compliment, looking uncomfortable.

"You, ornery?" I smiled.

"Yeah ..." she started to say, then stopped and put her hands on the dash, her head swiveling to follow a small black car that sped by us. "That's the Bailey boys!"

"It is!" I watched them disappear in my rearview mirror. "What're they doing out here? They're not supposed to leave Harmony, are they?"

"I don't know, but that's one too many coincidences."

"What do you mean?"

"First you see Samuel turn down their road; then you see him last night right after the Bailey boys leave; and now this. They're up to something, and Samuel is involved. I know it."

"Intuition?" I stared over at her.

"You got that right."

"So, now what do we do?"

"I'm not sure."

"Haven't channeled that message yet?"

She narrowed her eyes then chuckled and wriggled her fingers at her head. "No, it's still coming through."

I laughed too, but then turned serious. "Finally time to tell Patrick?"

"Yeah. It's time."

CHAPTER TWELVE

When Dori and I stepped into Patrick's office, Luke was sitting in a chair under the window with his head buried in a large book. Patrick was behind his desk. He and Dori had arranged for her to pick Luke up there late in the afternoon, knowing they'd be gone all day. Luke didn't look up as we walked over to Patrick's desk.

"How'd he do?" Dori asked quietly.

"It went fine. He asks a lot of questions."

"No kidding." She smiled.

"But, they're good questions." He smiled back. "He'd make a great forensic detective."

"Hey, Luke," Dori called to him, "come tell us about your day."

Lifting his head, he noticed us for the first time. "What?"

"Come over here."

Keeping the book open, he balanced it on his palms. "I need something to mark my spot," he said to Patrick when he reached the desk.

"What's that?" Dori asked as Patrick handed Luke a piece of scratch paper to slide into the book.

"A mug book. Deputy Crane wants me to find criminals we can link to the murder at the Bliss Mine."

"The office has a collection going way back. I'm having him take a look at the ones from the late nineties, when the murder occurred."

"Did you find any clues up there?" I directed my question at Luke.

"Yes. Yes, we did." Luke nodded his head, becoming animated. "Show them, Deputy Crane. Show them what we found."

Patrick held up a large plastic bag that was sitting on the corner of his desk. "This was just inside the entrance to a drift."

"It's a piece of cloth torn from a shirt that looks like it was there for a long time," Luke interjected. "There's probably more evidence down the drift, but Deputy Crane said we couldn't go in."

"What's a drift?" Dori asked.

"It's a horizontal tunnel," Luke answered. "A vertical tunnel's called a shaft."

"I didn't want to take a chance on that drift." Patrick set the bag down. "The support timbers looked safe, but that mine's been there a long time."

"Deputy Crane's going to send it to a lab to be analyzed." Luke patted the bag like it was a pet puppy.

"Well, that's cool," said Dori. "What do you expect to find out?"

"They can tell about the fibers, and if there's blood and hair they'll get DNA evidence for sure," Luke answered.

"Very cool."

"That's not all. We also found evidence of recent activity." Luke had moved into full on reporter mode.

"Someone else has been exploring the mine?" I looked at Patrick.

"Yeah, and ..." Luke interrupted again.

"Let Deputy Crane answer." Dori put her hand on Luke's shoulder.

"More like living there. We found a lot of trash, a sleeping bag, and evidence of a recent campfire."

"Who'd camp out in an old mine this time of year?" I asked.

"Mine temperature is consistent year round, so weather's not a factor, and a lot of people believe there are still valuable minerals in them to be had."

"Gold fever?" I said.

"Something like that."

"We'll get out of your hair now." Dori moved her hand to Luke's back.

Catching her eyes, I widened mine, wondering why we were leaving before telling Patrick we saw the Bailey boys.

"Thanks again for taking Luke." Dori ignored me. "Say good-bye and thank you, Luke."

"Can I come back tomorrow to finish the mug books?" he asked instead.

"No. I've got something I'm working on tomorrow. But, you can come by on Tuesday morning. I'll be here, catching up on paperwork. Sound good?"

"Yeah. That will be good."

"You're sure you want him here while you're working?" Dori asked.

"It's fine. I can use his help on the mug books, and if I get called out I'll send him along."

"Why didn't we tell Patrick about the Bailey boys?" I asked when we got outside and Luke was out of earshot.

"The mine."

"Yeah?"

"Don't you see? Samuel and the other men could've left that stuff there. It could be one of their hideouts."

"That's reaching, Dori. And if it *is* Samuel, that's even more reason to tell Patrick. We're not going to nose around a mine by ourselves."

Dori stared at me.

"Dori? Tell me you're not thinking about having us go up to that mine."

"We don't have to snowshoe. There's a gravel road."

"Yeah. And the possibility of dangerous men at the end of it. I'd like to live long enough to watch my hair turn gray."

"I don't see you ever letting that happen."

"Maybe not. Gray streaks don't blend well with red, but still ..."

"We're doing it for Angela. We'll go straight up and back. Two hours, tops."

"Oh, great. Use guilt." I shifted my eyes to a truck driving by then back to Dori. "Okay, fine, but it's going to have to wait 'til Tuesday. I need to write that article and get it off to Vincent, and I've got an editing deadline coming up."

"But Angela ..."

"I care about Angela too, but I need my day job. It's gotta be Tuesday and it's gotta be a quick trip, right?"

"Right." She didn't argue. "Pick me up at nine. We'll drop Luke off here and be on our way." She turned to catch up with Luke. "Thanks." She called over her shoulder.

Dori was a bossy one, but after hearing about her childhood I was sure her assertive streak is what saved her.

I had been at my computer so long my eyes were crossed. Sliding out of the dinette, I stood and stretched my arms up, touching the ceiling then glanced down at Mr. Bumbles, who was plopped down beside me. He had opened one eye to see what all the excitement was about, so I bent down to scratch him behind the ear. "Good old Uncle Malachi better catch the bad guys pretty soon, because this motorhome thing is getting really old." Although, it wasn't like I had to sleep or shower in it with Noah so accommodating.

Mr. B responded by shifting his weight onto his short legs and giving me his hopeful look, which is kind of like a smile with a lot of tongue involvement. It was dinnertime, the highlight of his day.

After I filled his bowl, I pulled out a bag of Fritos for myself and munched on them as I inspected the cupboards and refrigerator for dinner ingredients. I hadn't seen Noah at all that day, which was probably for the best. We had eaten together almost every night since my return and pretty much slept together as well. I wasn't complaining, mind you.

Pulling a package of tamales out of my tiny freezer, I started to read the cooking instructions when there was a knock on the door. Mr. B beat me to it, and I had to nudge him out of the way to open it. Standing there was Noah, with two horses in tow. Okay?

"I need to check on the calves in the far pasture. Thought you might like to ride along." He resettled his cowboy hat on his head.

"Isn't it going to be dark soon?"

"We've got at least an hour of daylight left and a lot of moon after that."

I stared from the tall, dark brown horse I'd seen Noah ride to the speckled gray one next to it. "The only horse I was ever on was a pony when I was about four, and I only know that because my parents kept a picture of it on their bookshelf."

"It's not hard."

Oh, boy. I liked animals and all, but using one for transportation was a whole other thing.

"The sun's not going to keep."

Where was my spirit of adventure? "Okay. Why not." I gestured with the tamales and the Fritos.

"You'll want to leave those behind." He grinned. "They'd make mounting the horse a little tough."

"Funny." I frowned at him and stepped back into the motorhome to put them away and grab my jacket.

Mounting proved a little tough, even without the Fritos. I think it had to do with my center of gravity. Once Noah gave my butt a shove or two, though, I felt pretty secure. That is, until we started to move. I couldn't seem to stop sliding sideways down the saddle. Oh well, it had to do, because Noah was getting pretty far ahead of me.

When he realized how far back I was, he halted his horse and waited for me to catch up.

"What are their names," I asked when I reached him and we were walking side by side.

"You're on Rosie, and this is Kahn. Rosie's my mom's horse. She's almost nineteen now, but she's sturdy."

"Good to know." Was that a reference to the padding on my hips that he was just shoving around?

As we left the ranch house grounds, we traveled in a direction opposite the road coming in from the highway. It was in the area where Noah's parents still stayed when they weren't in St. George and a part of the ranch I'd never seen. The air was chilly, but my jacket kept me comfy. Underneath that big apricot sky and next to Noah, I felt wrapped in a whisper-soft world.

When we passed by his parents' home, he pointed out the window of the bedroom that was his until he left for college and the fence he fell from and broke his wrist when he was six. The warmth of his voice said that his was a happy childhood. I understood how living among the sage-laced desert, cottonwood canyons, and cattle, untouched by the events taking place on the other side of his distant fences could help make it so.

We had come upon a huge pasture dotted with cattle. Noah stopped and slid from his horse. "Go ahead and dismount. We'll go a piece on foot."

Fine by me. I'd only been on Rosie a short while and my tailbone was already calling for a break. I rested my weight on the right stirrup and started to lift my left leg over the horse.

"Wrong side. Rosie won't like it." Noah dropped Kahn's reins and walked over. "Grab her mane and the reins in your left hand."

"She'll like that?"

"It's what she's used to." He patted her neck. "Grab the swell."

"The what?"

"The part of the saddle under the horn–with your right hand, if you need extra support. Now rest your weight on the left stirrup and pivot your right foot over her rear."

Great. I shifted my right leg over as instructed, but with my long arms and legs draped over her and my weight distributed down the entire length of her back it felt like I was about to settle in for a nap. Poor Rosie.

"Okay now, keep your right foot coming." I could tell from Noah's voice he was trying to suppress a laugh. I was glad he found it so entertaining.

As I did, I put so much pressure on the stirrup with my left foot that it started to push outward and Rosie shifted under me. "Oh, no!" Feeling like I was going to fall, I gripped even tighter to her mane.

"Whoa." Noah steadied her and rubbed her neck. "I've got her. Drop your right foot to the ground, and let up on her mane and the swell. You don't have to hang on so tight anymore." He was really having fun now, no longer able to contain his laughter. Sadist.

It felt good to have my right foot on the ground–finally–only my left foot was still stuck in the stirrup and I wasn't sure how long I could hold on before I ended up dangling upside down from it.

Noah put the flat of his palm into my back. "Use your right hand to lift your left foot out of the stirrup."

It worked. Yay. I handed Rosie's reins to Noah. "That was easy." I laughed too. It must have looked absolutely ridiculous. "Thank God you aren't into posting videos on the Internet. I'd never live it down."

After Noah loosely tied Rosie and Kahn's reins to a cottonwood tree, we walked from pair to pair of cows with their calves. For each calf, Noah rubbed his hand over its side, down its legs, and inspected its eyes. As he did so, he explained that their ranch was a cow-calf operation, with about a hundred cows at any time. The cows calved in the fall and he only kept the calves until they were weaned nine months later. Then they were sold to a feedlot.

When we had circled back to the horses, Noah untied Rosie's reins and handed them to me. "Hey, I just realized, you get to be here for the branding party." His eyes shined with enthusiasm. "It's this weekend."

"What's a branding party?"

"It's when we vaccinate, brand and castrate the calves."

"Oh, good." I was not nearly as enthusiastic.

"It's a big to-do. Lots of folks come. There's a barbeque."

"So basically, you throw a party for people to watch calves have their testicles removed? Fun."

"It is." He grinned. "You'll see."

"If you say so."

He held Rosie steady as I mounted her. "There's just enough daylight left for you to be introduced to Manny, Moe, Jack and Jim."

"Huh?"

"The boys."

"Okay?" Did he have ranch hands stashed away in some bunkhouse I'd never seen?

"Our bulls."

"Oh." Oh. The cows and calves were one thing, but I wasn't sure how close I wanted to get to a bull. "You sure they want to meet *me*?"

"Definitely."

When we reached the pasture where Noah kept his bulls, we fortunately stayed on the other side of the fence. They looked huge and cranky. He pointed them out by name, and told me they were prizewinners in the insemination department. He was particularly proud of Moe, who had impregnated twenty-nine cows last season. He also told me that if I were still around in December, I'd get to see them put the bulls on the cows, as in watch those giant beasts have their way with the poor unsuspecting females. Lucky me.

We made our way back to the ranch house, the air crisp and tangy and the wind beginning to stir the cottonwood leaves. Noah looked over and studied my face, then he smiled, just with his eyes.

There was no denying it. There were things about life in Harmony that were very good.

After we halted our horses outside the barn next to the house, I managed to dismount Rosie without incident. It gave me that same sense of self-confidence about handling ranch life as I had when I helped V.A. with the calving. More like delusion. In that instance, I ended up in cow poop with a very sore tailbone. One trip round the ranch on Rosie had not made me a cowgirl. I needed to keep that in mind.

Helping Noah remove the saddles, we put Kahn and Rosie into their stalls. He told me he wanted them in for the night, because the wind was picking up and it was supposed to be very cold. He also told me that I needed to find a safe place out of the wind and cold for the night, and he knew the exact spot.

Hot soup and sourdough bread; a warm fire and flannel sheets—and Noah. Peculiar old Harmony felt pretty close to heaven on that cold winter night.

CHAPTER THIRTEEN

The next morning as Dori and I pulled up in front of Patrick's office to drop Luke off, Genevieve screeched in behind us, barely missing the back end of our car before she slammed on the brakes. Wouldn't Cal have loved that one; yet another dent in the hatchback.

As Dori started to let Luke out of the back seat, we watched Genevieve march past us at a butt-bouncing clip. When she reached Patrick's office door, she grabbed the knob to throw it open in dramatic Genevieve fashion, but it was locked. Rapping on the door, she called Patrick's name. He didn't answer.

My curiosity aroused, I got out of the car and stood by the door, but didn't join Dori and Luke, who walked over to Genevieve. Turning her back on them, she pulled her cellphone from her massive purse and pressed the buttons.

Dori looked over at me and shrugged her shoulders. Luke walked up to the office window, cupped his hands around his eyes and pressed them to the glass. "He's not there." I heard him tell Dori.

Giving Genevieve's back a hard stare, Dori then turned to Luke and gestured for them to return to the car. Just as we were about to get back in, Patrick pulled his cruiser around in front of us and cut the engine.

Genevieve hurried over to him, blocking his exit from the car as he started to get out. "A fine deputy you are," she said.

Ignoring her, he set his long legs on the ground and stood up, towering over her.

"Why didn't you answer my emergency call?" She took a step back so she could dart arrows into his eyes rather than his chest. "The whole town could fall apart by the time you show up."

"I was on a call, Mrs. Bailey."

"It couldn't have been as important as the kidnapping of my sons!"

"Floyd and Lloyd have been kidnapped?" Patrick let just a tinge of disbelief into his voice. Who could blame him? The woman was a whack job.

Genevieve picked up on it. "You doubt me! Fine! Get me the number of a deputy in St. George who has some balls. Every minute you stand here like some dumb oaf puts the lives of my boys at risk!"

Genevieve may have gone a step too far with that one. Patrick shifted his service belt on his hips and crossed his arms. When he didn't speak right away, I wondered if he was counting to ten to calm his ire. I sure would have been. "Let's talk about this in the office, Mrs. Bailey," he said, without a trace of anger. Impressive.

"No. I'm not going to waste another minute with you. Just give me the number in St. George."

"If that's how you want it, Mrs. Bailey, but before that, can you identify this sweatshirt?" Patrick leaned into the cruiser and pulled out a large clear plastic bag containing a thick black hoodie with graphics on the sleeves. One of those sleeves was torn from the shoulder to the cuff.

"My God!" Genevieve wailed. "It's Lloyd's! I knew it! I knew it! A mother's instinct! My babies *have been* kidnapped!" She reached out to grab the jacket from Patrick's hand, but he lifted it out of her reach.

"Give that to me! Where did you find it?"

"There was another theft of copper last night. It was hanging from a barbed wire fence at the crime scene."

"Oh my, God! Criminals got them! You need to go after them, now!"

Oh my, God was right. How could she be so dense as to miss the obvious? Her precious little darlings *were* the criminals. I looked over at Dori, who nodded at me to get into the car.

"I'm not going to continue this out here, Mrs. Bailey. Let's go into the office, so I can take down your statement. If you still want to call St. George then I'll dial the number for you." There was no doubt in his voice that he would be more than happy to pass Genevieve off to some unsuspecting deputy.

Looking over at us, Patrick said to Luke, "We're going to have to put the mug books off until later in the day, Luke. Can you check back with me after lunch?"

"Yeah, I guess."

"It's okay, Lucas," Dori said to him. "You can help Dusty with the morning and lunch shifts. We'll go back and grab your video games for when it's slow."

"That would be good." He nodded enthusiastically. Nothing like an electronic device to improve a teenager's outlook.

Starting up the same highway we had driven on Sunday, Dori informed me we weren't going to the Bliss Mine after all. Emmet had called her from his cousin's cellphone the previous afternoon to say he had seen some men drive by his cabin who might be Samuel and his buddies.

"And you didn't tell Patrick? Why?" I asked. "If they're up there, Patrick and an army of deputies need to go after them, not us. We can't do anything on our own, without being maimed or killed, that is."

"We'll just drive as far as Emmet's, and if it does turn out to be Samuel, we'll call Patrick from there."

"Two things wrong with your scheme, and you know it. This isn't exactly a four-wheel drive car, and Samuel may recognize it."

"Emmet said they plowed the road. And we can hide the car behind the cabin."

"You thought of everything." I frowned at her. "It's still too dangerous."

"Not really. Our best chance of catching them and getting Angela back is to figure out where they are and let Patrick know, so he can sneak up on them and nab them."

"I didn't think you watched TV."

"What do you mean?"

"You sound like a bad actress from a B-rated detective show."

"No." That one made her smile.

"Yes." I smiled back.

"Come on, Syd. We'll be safe at Emmet's."

"That's right. We've got all those rocks to protect us. Only they're a little small to knock someone out."

"This can work." Her tone was so confident she almost made me believe it.

"Fine."

The plowed road made it an easy ride to Emmet's house. I parked the car at the back between two tall spruce trees, so it would be hard to spot. When we stepped onto the porch, we noticed the door to the cabin was open a crack. Dori pushed on it and called Emmet's name, but he didn't answer. We waited a few beats, called his name again, and when he didn't come decided to venture in.

"Emmet," Dori said loudly as she crossed the room and reached the bedroom door. When he didn't respond, she opened it and peeked her head in. "No sign of him." She looked back at me.

"The fire's cold." I poked the ashes with a long stick I found on the hearth. "You think his cousin could have taken him shopping or something?"

"He wouldn't have left his door open, and check out this coat and cap." She walked back over to the entrance and ran her hand down the sleeve of a long wool coat that was hanging on a hook. "He would have worn a coat if he went out."

"Maybe he has another one."

"No. Something's happened to him." She put her hands on her waist and surveyed the room. "Look at this." She walked over to the log table next to his wicker rocking chair. It was lying on its side. "Something definitely happened to him." She picked his turquoise rock off the floor and held it up to me.

"Samuel?" I stepped over and took the turquoise from her.

"Yeah." She stood up and started for the door.

"Where are you going?"

"We need to walk up the road and see if there are any signs of them."

"They'll spot us."

"We'll use the trees for cover."

I looked down at my feet. "We didn't dress to go tramping through the snow."

"We'll be fine. We need to go–now. Who knows what they might do to Emmet."

"I'm only coming if you call Patrick. It's time to tell him what we're up to, Dori." I crossed my arms.

Pressing her lips together, she stared at me. "You're right," she sighed, finally giving in.

During Dori's conversation with Patrick, he told her to stay put in Emmet's cabin. Like that was going to happen. When she clicked off, she told me we would just take a quick peek up the road and come right back. Right.

There was snow piled up to the porches and the walks hadn't been shoveled on the first three cabins we checked out from behind the trees that lined the road. The path to the fourth cabin hadn't been cleared either, but there were deep footprints leading to the door.

"Let's circle around the back and see if there's anyone in there," Dori whispered to me.

"But there aren't any cars."

"Those footprints are fresh."

"So, now you're a scout? How do you know?" I frowned at her.

"They'd be covered with snow if they were old. Come on." She crouched and walked beyond the cabin then circled around to the back of it.

I followed, shivering in my soaked tennis shoes, thinking I'd be lucky if I didn't end up with frostbite.

Bending very low, we moved quickly to a small window. Dori lifted her head just high enough to look through it then pointed her finger at the other window and crouched over to it. I followed, my thighs burning and back aching. I still hadn't recovered from our Sunday jaunt, and there I was, once again, in ankle-deep snow.

One glance into the second window and Dori dropped right back down, putting her finger to her lips. "Someone's in there," she mouthed.

"What do we do?" I mouthed back.

Lifting her head back up, she stared for so long I was worried she was going to get caught. "Emmet's tied up in there!" she whispered loudly. "I don't think anyone's with him. Let's try the back door." She moved over to it before I could reach out to stop her. If Emmet was tied up, there had to be someone watching him, and Dori was going to walk right into him!

Turning the knob, Dori opened the door wide enough for her head to fit through and waited. When she didn't hear anything, she turned to me and pantomimed, "Wait here. Call Patrick if there's trouble." What was she thinking? Patrick was still a long way away. How could *he help*?

Stepping slowly into the house, she pulled the door closed, but didn't let it latch shut. I moved over to the window and lifted my head high enough to look in. I didn't see anything at first then noticed movement to my right. Dori crept over to the entry to the living room where there was someone sitting on the floor with his back to the wall. I thought it was Emmet. It was hard to tell. He had thin gray hair, anyway.

After staying hidden for another minute, she walked quickly over to Emmet. When no one leaped up to tackle her,

I hurried into the cabin. By the time I got to them, Dori had Emmet almost completely untied. He was looking a little dazed, but didn't seem to be hurt.

"Let's get you into the chair," Dori was saying to him as she gently took his arm and helped him to his feet.

With his hands shaking, Emmet stood for a few moments to steady himself, then allowed Dori to assist him into a worn leather chair.

"Would you get him a glass of water?" Dori turned to me.

When I came back with it from the kitchen, Dori was seated on a wooden folding chair close to Emmet, her hand on his. I took a seat on the fireplace hearth nearby.

"What happened?" Dori asked him after he had taken a few sips of water.

"After I called you yesterday, I meandered up the road to get a closer look. I noticed two young men watching me from the porch and I thought it best to get back home. I had only been there a few minutes when they came through the door, grabbed me, and dragged me to their car. I put up a fight, mind you, but my limbs aren't as strong as they used to be." He took another sip of water and handed the glass to Dori, who set it on the ground.

"We think we know who those boys are. Did they have long dark bangs that hang over their eyes and drive a small black car in need of a paint job?" Dori asked.

He nodded.

"Were there men with them?"

"Oh, yes. It was a full cast of villains." Despite being in his nineties and having spent the night on the floor, Emmet was recovering quickly. His hands had steadied and his voice was strong.

"Did it include a man with a large head and thick stubby legs, kind of like Popeye?" I asked. "Did you hear the name Samuel?"

"No. I didn't hear any names, but yes," his eyes smiled at me, "there was indeed a Popeye character."

"Was a little blonde girl with him?" Dori spoke up.

"Yes. They had her in the bedroom. I only saw the back of her as they were leaving."

My stomach knotted as I caught the worried look on Dori's face. "Was anyone else with them?"

"Yes. There were two other men, tough guys."

"Why did they leave you here?" I asked.

"I'll be happy to tell you the whole story, young ladies, but I think it'd be wise for us to get back to my cabin first."

"Of course!" I said, suddenly a lot more conscious that we were all still in danger.

Since Emmet couldn't move quickly, I decided to run to his cabin to get the car and his coat and come back for him and Dori. When we got back there, Emmet settled into his rocker, tucked his hands in his pockets and gave us a brief account of what had happened.

When the Bailey boys brought Emmet to the cabin, Samuel was there with the other men. Emmet had no idea at the time they were hiding Angela in the bedroom. After they tied him up, they grilled him about what'd he seen and who he'd told. He admitted nothing. But Samuel, in particular, didn't believe him. He told the men to get rid of him, kill him if they had to. They didn't take it well. They told him he wasn't the boss and accused him of trying to take over their operation. They exchanged heated words, with their hands on the guns in their belts. All the while, the Bailey boys stood trying to fade into the background, looking scared enough to shit their pants. Emmet's words–and good to hear. They deserved it.

It was decided they'd leave Emmet there and move to their other hideout. While they were preparing to leave and with their tempers still flaring, the men told Samuel that after that night he was on his own. And if he didn't pay them the money he owed them and light out for Mexico like he'd been telling them, *he'd* be the dead one.

Before they walked out the door, they warned Emmet they'd be back to deal with him later.

And now it was later. And time for us to get out of there. Emmet agreed he should leave with us. When Samuel's gang found out he'd escaped, his cabin was the first place they'd look. Patrick would be arriving on the scene anytime, but there'd be nothing to see. They'd call him from the road and fill him in.

CHAPTER FOURTEEN

While I navigated the curvy mountain roads, driving as fast as I could without careening off a cliff, Dori called Patrick. She'd been relegated to the backseat so Emmet didn't have to twist himself into it. Just as Patrick answered, I spotted his car in my rearview mirror on the switchback below us. I told Dori to let him know I'd pull over so we could meet up.

We filled him in about Emmet and our suspicions that Samuel and the men were using the Bliss Mine as a hideout. Patrick immediately put his car in gear and picked up his radio. He told us he was calling for backup. He also told us we should head back to Harmony and he'd fill us in when he got there. He wanted Emmet to hang around town long enough to give his statement. Then Patrick rolled up his window, maneuvered his car into a tight U-turn and sped away.

Dori, who was propped on the edge of the back seat with her head between Emmet's and mine, looked from one to the other of us. "His backup's going to be a longtime coming."

"And?" I said.

"The Bliss Mine. What do you think, Emmet? Should we follow Patrick there?"

Sure. Ask the new guy. She already knew *my answer*.

"In for a penny; in for a pound." Emmet gripped the cane he had brought along with him and tapped it on the floorboard as if he was making a formal proclamation.

"Great! You in, Syd?"

"Would it matter?"

"Not so much." Dori scooted back and reattached her seatbelt.

"We're protected." Emmet stared out the front window.

Good to know. He must have been wearing one of his lucky rocks. I stared at Dori in the rearview mirror. She was fingering the lapis pendant she'd been wearing ever since Emmet gave it to her. I had left my rhodonite necklace on a shelf in the RV. I wondered if that was grounds to kick me out of the club.

As we approached the mine, we heard faint popping sounds over the crunch of gravel under our tires. "That's gunshots!" Dori grabbed the back of my seat. "Stop the car!"

I pulled to the edge of the road, my heart pounding, and killed the engine, feeling very vulnerable with as few trees as there were in the area around the mine.

"Patrick's there alone. We need to see if we can help him." Dori unbuckled her seatbelt.

Emmet started to open his door.

"Wait!" I said. "Shouldn't we have a plan?"

Dori drummed the back of my seat. "Okay, Emmet, here's my cellphone. Put in a call to emergency. Tell them shots have been fired and ask how long it'll be 'til backup arrives. Syd, let's you and I get as close as we can. If Patrick's got it under control, we go in. Otherwise, we wait for help."

"Okay," I said, relieved that Dori was finally using caution.

When Dori and I came within sight of the mine, but were still quite a distance away, we squatted down next to a large thorny bush. Patrick's car was parked across the entrance to the mine with the driver's door open. There was a still figure lying face down a few feet from the rear of the car. Patrick was crouched by the open door with a gun in his hand. No one else was visible. I had just put my hand on Dori's arm to signal we should get out of there when the Bailey boys streaked around the hood of Patrick's car, headed our direction. Patrick lifted his gun as if to shoot, but instead stared down the barrel then lowered his weapon.

Dori and I only had a few seconds to plan our move before the Bailey boys were on us. "Let's trip 'em. You take Lloyd," she whispered. "I'll take Floyd."

"Which one's Lloyd?" I whispered back.

"Black shirt."

Neither one of them saw us until they were right on top of us. Floyd hit the gravel so hard it was like he had taken a high dive into a waterless pool, courtesy of a sharp kick by Dori. I stuck my foot out to trip Lloyd right after that, but he didn't stay down long and was off again before I could stop him. He didn't get far, though. Emmet hadn't stayed in the car after all. He appeared like magic out of the bushes and whipped his cane right into the center of Lloyd's belly before he knew what hit him. Lloyd doubled over, gasping for air, then rolled to his side and curled up like a baby. A wonderful sight to see!

The commotion with Floyd and Lloyd drew Patrick's attention and he motioned for us to stay back then gestured to the mine.

"There must be more people in there!" Dori sat down on top of Floyd when he started to stir. "Quick, can you find something in the car to tie them up?"

"I'll look. Are you okay with Lloyd, Emmet?" I asked.

"He's not going anywhere." Emmet poked him with his cane. Lloyd curled up even tighter.

Staying low and hurrying to my car, I found an old thin towel of Cal's tucked in the cargo area. Tearing it in strips as I rushed back, I handed them a few at a time to Emmet. He pieced them together and bound the boys' hands and feet with knots so perfect he could've earned a merit badge.

"I hope Angela's okay," Dori said from her perch on Floyd.

"I know. How Samuel could subject her to all this is insane." Emmet and I were now squatted down next to Dori. Feeling the burn in my thighs, I wondered how Emmet managed it. He was one resilient old guy.

We watched as Patrick knelt and opened the back car door, reached in and started to grab something out. Shots suddenly rang out in rapid fire. We buried our heads in our arms and bent low to the ground. After a minute and just as we were about to lift them, more shots shattered the air and blasted gravel so close to us I felt a stinging in my legs and arms. When we uncovered our eyes long enough to check on Patrick, he was moving toward the trunk of the car. Raising his gun, he fired several shots into the tunnel then sat back down and leaned against the rear tire.

"How much ammunition do you think Patrick's got," I mumbled, my head still face down.

"Not much." Emmet said.

When I glanced at him, I noticed a trickle of blood running down from his hairline. "You're hurt, Emmet."

"Just a nick." He fingered the wound. "Heads bleed a lot."

"Hey, I'm bleedin' too!" It was Floyd. There were several nicks on his cheek and the blood was dripping into the gravel. "I need to get to an emergency room!"

"Fine. Why don't you just stand right up and head for the car. The keys are still in the ignition." Dori shifted off him, still staying low to the ground. "Go ahead. We'll watch as your buddy shoots you down."

"Maybe I will. He won't shoot me."

"Oh, that's right, on account of how much he cares about you."

Floyd mustered a hard stare at Dori, but didn't try to get up.

"Change your mind?"

"You can't treat us like this!" He strained at the ties around his wrists. "My mom's gonna sue you!"

"You ever get tired of saying that?" I asked.

"Well, she is." He sneered at me.

"Hey, Floyd," Dori said. "Who's in the mine?"

"Seth."

"Shut up, Floyd," Lloyd gasped out, still lying on his side. "Don't tell 'em nothin'."

"Samuel and Angela aren't in there with them, Floyd?" Dori grabbed him by the hair and tugged.

"Ouch! Stop it!" He twisted his body, trying to pull away from her.

"Don't say nothin'," Lloyd warned his brother again.

"He doesn't have to." She let go of Floyd. "There's gotta be only one of them left in there," she said to us. "Samuel must have escaped with Angela."

"Yeah, and he didn't pay up! He's dead meat!" Floyd lifted his head.

"Shut up, Floyd!" His brother came up on his elbow.

Shots rang out again in rapid-fire succession, spraying so much gravel it took a few moments for the air to clear of dust. When we could see again, Patrick was still sitting against the car and a man with a long dark beard was standing on the other side of it. Since Patrick made no move to return fire, he was definitely out of bullets. We watched in horror as the man bent over and began to inch his way around the rear of the car, his gun drawn.

Patrick backed around the open car door toward the engine, the only protection he had, and not likely to stop a bullet.

"We've got to do something!" I gripped Dori's arm.

"But, we don't have any weapons!" Dori looked desperately around. "And, once he's killed Patrick, he'll come after us! Our only chance is to break for the car when he starts shooting." She looked from me to Emmet.

"But Patrick," I said.

"I know, but we can't help him. I die, Lucas is left with no one. I'm not doing that to him." Dori stared me down.

I nodded, staring back.

"Get positioned to run." Dori shifted to her haunches. "The second you hear a shot–go!"

"What about us?" Floyd's voice shook with fear.

"You made your own beds, boys." Emmet put his hand on Lloyd. "If you survive this, remember that. Every step you took was *your choice*."

Lloyd cast his eyes up at Emmet then squeezed them shut. A tear streaked through the grime on his cheek.

Keeping my eyes on the man's dark head as it continued to move closer to Patrick, I prayed like I never had before. When it disappeared completely, I held my breath, waiting for an arm to reach around and blast Patrick with a hail of bullets. Then the loud peal of sirens pierced the air, and the man popped up and darted back into the mine. A few seconds later, two sheriff's cars squealed to a stop next to us. Using their engines as shields, they got out and crouched behind the front of the car. The deputy closest to us called out asking how many men had Patrick pinned down. We told him we thought only the one, but couldn't be sure.

"Drop your weapon, put your hands on your head and walk out of there, now! You've got nowhere to go!" the other deputy shouted.

When there was no movement from the mine, he said, "We can starve you out if you wanna play it that way. We've got all the time in the world."

When the man still didn't appear, he said, "Don't wanna come out yet. Fine by us. In the meantime, it looks like your buddy there may not be able to hang on as long, if he's not dead already. You want his death on your head, do ya?"

After a couple of tense minutes, the man moved from the dark of the mine into the light, and the deputies next to us readied their weapons.

"Hands folded on top of your head, and move around the hood of the car, real slow," the one near us said in a loud but even tone.

Patrick scooted toward the trunk as the man started to move slowly along the front bumper.

"That's right. Keep coming."

As he got closer, the deputies from the other vehicle pointed their guns at him and approached. "Stay there, and keep those hands where I can see 'em," one of them called out.

When they reached him, they drew his hands around his back and handcuffed him. He looked over at Patrick, who was leaning over the still body, then was led away.

"This your idea of heading back to Harmony?" Patrick asked as we watched the ambulance depart and the Bailey boys and the man who had been captured drive off in the back of the sheriffs' vehicles. "You ever do what you're told?"

It had been a crazy scene for almost an hour as the deputies sorted out the captives and searched the mine, and the paramedics tended to the wounded man. Well back from the action, we heard them tell Patrick that the guy had lost a lot of blood, but he should pull through.

"If we hadn't been here, the Bailey boys would've escaped." Dori defended our actions.

"You think they'd get far on foot up here?" Patrick didn't seem impressed at all by our heroics.

"Who are those guys?" I asked, deciding it best to change the subject.

"Brothers. Seth and Reed Midgeman. Several departments have been tracking them for months. They're the ones heading up the metal theft racket in the area."

"And the Bailey boys?"

"Working for them as grunts. Getting caught is the best thing that ever happened to them. They were ripe for disposal."

"What do you mean by that?"

"We all know they're screwups. Lloyd left his jacket at the last theft site. It'd only take something like that to get back to Seth and Reed and those boys would disappear forever–probably down one of those shafts." Patrick pointed his thumb at the mine.

My scalp prickled on that news. I wasn't fond at all of Floyd and Lloyd, but being tossed down a mineshaft? Yikes!

"I've gotta get back," Patrick stared down the road. "I'm going to be burning the midnight oil with the paperwork on this one. I'll get that statement from you first though, Emmet, so you don't have to ride all the way down to Harmony and back. I'll follow you to his place," Patrick glanced over at me.

When we walked into Emmet's cabin, it was so cold we could see our breath. Emmet immediately went to the hearth and started stacking logs on the grate, but Dori insisted he sit down in his willow rocker and let her do it. She assigned me to tea brewing.

By the time I finished my task, Dori had the fire blazing, a survival skill she said she learned at a very young age. Not for use on happy little camping trips, but because she was in charge of the household wood stove. If she let it go out, the punishment was swift and severe. Would I love to give her parents a taste of swift and severe. They ranked right up there with Samuel Vaullie.

After handing a cup of tea to Emmet, I set one in front of Patrick, who was perched on a bench at the table, looking much like a heron on a twig.

"I'll get your statements in town." Patrick looked up at me, his pen poised over his notebook, ready for us to leave so he could get down to business.

"You'll tell him everything you remember about Samuel and Angela, right Emmet?" Dori touched her hand to his shoulder.

"Yes." He patted the back of her hand. "You'll get her back."

"Okay," she sighed. "Okay."

Back in Harmony, Dori and I grabbed a bite to eat at Dusty's. The day felt like it had gone on forever and it was only three o'clock. I hung around town until Patrick returned and the two of us gave him our statements. Dori had already told Patrick back at the Bliss Mine that Samuel was on his way to Mexico and that Angela would disappear forever if they made it across the border. Slapping her hand on Patrick's desk for emphasis, she asked that he put pressure on Mother Helen to find out if she knew where they went. He reassured her they were doing everything they could to find him.

Naturally, Dori wasn't satisfied. Turns out she had a cousin in a polygamist community in Chihuahua, Mexico, and she planned to contact her. Where *didn't* Dori have a cousin? With polygamists, they sprouted up like dandelion weeds.

CHAPTER FIFTEEN

Making my way to the branding party, I walked along the ranch road where Noah and I had ridden a few days before. As I passed Manny, Moe, Jack, and Jim's pasture, they were standing in their respective corners, their hulking heads lowered slightly and their eyes fixed straight ahead. They looked like heavyweight champs staring down their challengers before the big fight. Intimidating. I was glad they were corralled behind a sturdy fence.

They didn't know how lucky they were to have missed their own castration celebration. Too bad about their bull calf buddies joining the day's festivities, though. The poor unsuspecting things had no idea when they woke up that morning that by the time the sun set they were going to be missing a couple of vital body parts and wearing a tattoo not of their own choosing.

Noah had reassured me that branding and castration were necessary parts of a cow-calf operation and the calves came through it just fine. I still had a hard time accepting the idea of a testicle-themed party. I doubted you could find any balloons or napkins for that.

Noah and I hadn't seen much of each other in the last few days. He had gone quiet when I told him that I'd been up at the Bliss Mine during the shootout with the Midgeman brothers. No reproach; no questions; just a long hard stare. Then, he reset his cowboy hat on his head and walked off to the barn. I didn't like that. It was a lot harder to take than an argument, but I left him alone. I had to work on my article for Vincent and my copy editing anyway. And I finished it all. It's amazing how much you can get done when the hair curling down a guy's neck isn't there to distract you.

The only distraction to my work had been the updates I received from Dori regarding Samuel and Angela and the metal theft arrests. Reed Midgeman had survived, but was still in intensive care. The arraignment for Seth Midgeman and the Bailey boys took place late the previous afternoon. Turns out Genevieve was going to have a hard time keeping her precious little darlings out of jail this time. Stealing metal made them petty thieves. Kidnapping Emmet made them felons–not something a judge or jury was going to take lightly. Their only hope was that they receive some leniency for agreeing to testify against the Midgemans. Even at that, though, they were going to be cowering behind bars for quite a while, and they couldn't be more deserving.

Samuel, evil wraith that he was, had disappeared. Dori expected that he and Angela were safely over the Mexican border by then. She, of course, had a plan she intended to explain to me at the party that afternoon. I was surprised to hear she was coming out to Noah's ranch for it, but then I realized I shouldn't have been. All events in Harmony seemed to be the *Y'all come!* type–like in the South–only this was Southern Utah. Yee haw!

Stuffing my hands into my pockets to ward off the cold, I rounded the last bend in the road to the corrals where Noah told me I'd find the party. I stopped to take in the scene, wondering how he thought I could possibly miss it. There were as many people in and around the corrals as at the round dance, and as many cows–all in motion!

There were cowboys on horseback outside the corrals herding heifers and calves into them; two women stoking a fire in a large oil drum; people tending a grill and fussing over a long table already stacked with bowls; and three guys pulling guitar cases out of the bed of a truck. Noah was standing over some kind of metal contraption in the middle of it all. As I got closer I realized there was a calf locked into it.

Not sure how or whether to go through the gate, I hesitated on the other side of it. Looking again at the women tending the fire, I realized it was Miriam and V.A. I raised my hand in greeting when they saw me. They waved heavily gloved hands back at me, then V.A. walked over.

"Come on in, Missy." She pulled off her glove, unlatched the gate and held it open.

"Thanks." I walked through and stood waiting for further instructions, feeling as out of place as a gorilla at Sunday night dinner.

"Gotta get back to the irons. Follow me." V.A. made her way to the oil drum in a few long strides.

"Hi, Miriam," I said, stepping in next to her. Her cheeks were red, but from the fire rather than the cold, and beads of perspiration had formed on her upper lip and forehead. "What's all this?" I looked down into the drum, where both Miriam and V.A. were holding the ends of iron rods and twisting them.

"These are the branding irons." Miriam pulled one out. The end was the color of light ash and shaped into the letter D with a small upside down letter T inside of it. "This one's the Thompson's."

"And this is ours." V.A. held up an iron with the letters S and L intertwined then glanced away, her attention diverted. "Noah's ready for me." She hurried over to him.

"Go on. See how it's done," Miriam encouraged me. "V.A.'s the best brander in the county."

"Okay." I shouldn't have been surprised.

Standing a few feet back from V.A. and Noah, I watched as she held the branding iron over the calf's haunches. Noah had one hand on the area behind the calf's head. The other hand held a syringe, which looked to me like it was large enough to vaccinate an elephant. V.A. brought the iron down on the calf and rocked it. Flames leapt up, followed by smoke and a smell that burned my nostrils. The calf moved. V.A. pulled the iron off. And it was all over in about five seconds. By the time I realized I had just witnessed fire shoot up from a baby cow, Noah had swung the metal cage to an upright position and released the calf. It was herded by a man I recognized as Noah's father, Wayne, to an adjacent corral and its waiting mother. Or, somebody's mother, anyway. Either way, it didn't seem too upset.

V.A. walked back to the oil drum and Noah had another calf squeezed into the metal cage and swung up on to its side right away. He nodded for me to come closer. It was the first I knew he'd even noticed me. I took a couple steps, but still hung back.

"Move on in here," he said without looking back. "You need to get a gander at the whole shebang."

"A gander at the whole shebang, huh?" I smiled as I stepped closer. "You talk like a character from an old Western."

"I talk like my grandad." His eyes smiled. "He had a lot of those expressions and was a *real* character."

"Is he the D in your brand?"

"Very good. Yeah. The Crazy Diederik Thompson."

"Crazy?"

"An upside down letter in a brand is called *crazy*. My grandad used to say he got the idea from folks telling him he was crazy for starting a cattle ranch on land this arid, but he did all right." Noah had a very sharp looking knife in his hand that he was moving around as he talked. I was glad I was still out of reach by the head of the calf. It was lying very still, but then it didn't have much choice with the way it was clamped in.

"What *is* this thing?" I touched one of the metal bars that held the calf.

"A calf table. It makes the job a lot easier than roping them and having to brand and castrate on the ground." He turned from me, grabbed the calf's testicles, and started slicing them off–just like that! No prelude. No warning.

I was speechless and would like to say disgusted, but that would be an exaggeration. Actually, I was impressed with Noah's speed and fluidity. Just as he was finishing, his mom appeared with a bowl in her hand.

"Sydney." She nodded at me then held the bowl out to Noah.

"Hi, Anne." I raised my hand. "Good to see you."

Noah tossed the testicles into the bowl, one that looked suspiciously like it had come out of Anne's kitchen. "What happens to those?" I looked at the contents.

"We eat them." Noah smiled. I bet he'd been anticipating for days the look on my face when he informed me of that little tidbit.

"*Really?*"

"You never heard of Rocky Mountain oysters?"

"That's what they call them? No. I've never seen them on a menu in my life. Does that somehow surprise you?"

"Mom's got a great recipe." He grabbed a can from the ground by his feet and started spraying the castration site on the calf with some kind of brown liquid. "Anti-bacterial solution," he said as a way of explanation.

"Come on with me," Anne spoke up. "I can use some prep help in the kitchen."

"Okay." What was this, some kind of test? If I'm willing to touch fresh calf balls I pass?

"Noah, tell Marge to bring the last of the testicles to me when you're through," she said as she turned to walk away.

"See you later," I said to Noah, widening my eyes in a *save me* signal.

He just winked, enjoying my discomfort way too much.

Anne and I took her truck back to their farmhouse and I was assigned the job of skinning the testicles and dropping them into a bowl of beer. After my initial revulsion at tackling the veiny slimy globs, I just thought, what the hell, I've eaten a lot of other cow parts, why not the nasty bits?

So, I passed. At least, I felt I had, until Anne started asking me about my childhood, my family, Los Angles, my work, my plans, and on and on. She hadn't seemed the prying type before, but then, she had to be wondering about the nature of my relationship with her son with my motorhome parked a few yards from his house. Not to mention my having been caught emerging from his bedroom wearing only my sweater. A mother's prerogative, I guess.

The nature of my relationship with Noah had been on my mind too—a lot. The desire to see his face, to be with him, was making it ever more difficult to envision a life without him in it. I needed to share that with him—soon—to find out if he felt the same way. Then I needed to begin reassembling the puzzle pieces of my future according to the outcome of the conversation. But, did I have the guts to have it? And, more importantly, was I certain of what I wanted the outcome to be?

By the time Anne and I got back to the branding party with testicles that had been sliced, breaded, and fried into much more appetizing Rocky Mountain oysters, even more people had arrived on the scene, including Dori and Luke. Patrick, Cal, and Lou had also shown up, and were huddled in conversation next to Lou's giant gray horse. I realized she must have been one of the "cowboys" I had seen herding the cattle. The way she sat a horse, it would be impossible to distinguish her from a man, and I'm sure she preferred it that way. She'd have made a great trail boss. Those cattle wouldn't dare get out of line, not to mention the cowpokes.

When Dori saw me arranging the bowls on the buffet table, she came right over. "Happy branding party," I said, reaching into the large cooler next to the table. "Beer?"

"No, thanks. I don't drink."

"Oh. That's right. I guess I've never seen you with a drink in your hand."

"Makes me feel too vulnerable."

"That's an interesting way to put it." I pulled out a beer for myself.

"Comes from seeing rebellious wives and daughters drugged to keep them in line."

"Wow! You never mentioned *that* before. Did they drug *you*?"

"No, but I'm sure they were considering it before I left."

"Jeez. The thing that continues to amaze me is that those men get away with such a smorgasbord of crimes! Where's the public outcry?"

"That's why you wrote your article, Syd. Remember? And that's why we're going to Mexico to make sure Samuel isn't one of the ones who gets away with it."

"We are?" I set my beer on the table.

"Yeah." She locked eyes with me. "I got a hold of my cousin and asked her to keep a lookout for Samuel. I told her what he's done."

"But didn't you say she's a practicing polygamist? Wouldn't she be on *his* side?"

"She told me that the people in her compound didn't want to have anything to do with Warren Jeffs and his followers when they were looking for a place to relocate, so they wouldn't be on Samuel's side either. And she's got a phone, a freedom I never would've been allowed."

"So, we're back to the whole good polygamist/bad polygamist argument, like with Miriam and Odelia?"

"No. There's no argument. It's all bad." She dug her fists into her waist. "But, we need their help."

"How's this going to work?" I rested my hip against the table. "I mean; we're going to drive right into Mexico and track Samuel down? Will the Mexican police even care if we *do* find him? What about the whole jurisdiction and extradition stuff?"

"We've got a long drive to figure it out."

"When are we leaving on this hot pursuit?"

"Tomorrow."

"Tomorrow!" I stood straight up.

"Yeah. You finished all that work you were worried about, and the longer we wait the less chance of finding Angela."

"Oh, boy, Dori." I ran my fingertips across my forehead. "You don't think this is going to be a wild goose chase?"

"I don't. Samuel's got nowhere else to go, and he doesn't know I warned her about him. I told my cousin if he shows up to take him in, pretend like they're happy to see him and we'd be there day after tomorrow. I also asked her not to say anything to anyone else about it."

"Can you trust her?"

"Yeah. I think so. It's been a long time since I've seen her, but we were pretty close when we were little."

"So, how far is this trek we're taking?"

"I don't know exactly; several hundred miles."

"Whoa."

"I know, but we'll take turns driving."

Staring over Dori's shoulder at the corral where Noah was tidying up from his branding marathon, I wondered how I was going to break this latest news to him. Oh, well. His reaction wouldn't have any influence on my decision to go anyway. Samuel was a psychopathic brute, who needed to be locked away. And I wanted the satisfaction of witnessing it. "Okay." I put my hand on Dori's arm. "We'll go, but we better talk to Cal about whether the little hatchback is up for yet another long road trip. I also think we should let Patrick in on our plans. He knows a heck of a lot more about the law than we do."

"Fine, but can we just wait 'til we're down there? I don't want him alerting the local police that we think Samuel may be in the area. At least, not until we know they're on our side."

When Dori and I walked over to talk to Cal about the car, fortunately Lou was busy seeing to her horse. The last thing I wanted was to provide the entertainment once again at a Harmony gathering by having her pick a fight with me. Cal didn't think there'd be any problem with the car, *no siree, Bob*. Like he'd told me before, she was a real gem—could run for another hundred thousand miles—but just to make sure, he'd check the oil and tire pressure on the way out this evening. What a guy. Lou didn't deserve him.

As the day slid into evening, the darkness pressed the branding party crowd into a tight band encircling a blazing fire. Perched on hay bales, their faces incandescent, the intermingled group of ranchers popped Rocky Mountain oysters and chewed on sweet smoked ribs from the plates perched on their laps. With their toes tapping to the guitarists' country tunes, their banter was punctuated with an occasional whoop of laughter that pierced the night sky. It was a scene as old as the West itself.

The intimacy of the gathering coupled with the chill at our backs, drew me to slide nearer to Noah on our hay bale. When he felt me press my thigh and shoulder into his, he wrapped his arm around my back and drew me even closer. Then he stared at me for a few long moments, his eyes soft. I set my hand on his thigh and returned his gaze. He gently kissed my forehead and pressed his hand into my back.

His touch and affection filled me–completely.

When he let go, I noticed that his parents, also sharing a bale, had been watching us. They smiled and raised their cups in a toast across the flames. I smiled and toasted back then looked over at Noah. He nodded his head at them and gave me another squeeze. Maybe I really did pass the test.

After the fire was doused, the horses trailered and the guests had caravanned out to the highway, I rode with Noah to his ranch house, bareback on Kahn. Was the moment real or alchemy–the transformation of red soil and jagged rocks into a billion glimmering crystals set in an obsidian sky? It was all so timeless–as if while I settled into the warmth of Noah's arms, Kahn gently walked us back through epochs, the muffled sound of his hoofs drumming the cadence.

When we reached the house, Noah slid off first then guided me down and turned me around by the waist when I reached the ground. Running his hand down my back, he drew me to him, lowered his head and touched his lips to mine, softly at first then with a hunger so overpowering that the only thing I was aware of was my own quickening desire.

When we finally pulled apart, I was breathing so hard I put my hand to my chest, as if to stop my heart from leaping out. I didn't talk. I knew if I had, that enchantment whirling around us would shatter. Noah wrapped his hand around mine and we led Kahn into the barn. I watched, leaning on the stall door as he bedded him down for the night.

Noah held my hand again as he guided me into the house and his bedroom. In the muted light, we made love deliberate and slow, our senses heightened to each movement. And when it was over, we still said nothing–just listened until the tides of the night and each other washed up into our dreams.

Coming out of those dreams, I awakened to the awareness that I was the only one in the bed. Rolling to my back, I stretched my spine and reached my arms up, touching the headboard with the tips of my fingers. Dropping them down, I curved my body into the pillow, reluctant to let go of the warmth and the sensations of the night before. Then my brain shot into gear and I sat up. "Bumbles and Alice!" Swinging my legs over the side of the bed, I reached for my clothes and started to throw them on.

"Bumbles is in the kitchen with Trudy, and Alice is sleeping in." Noah pushed the door open with his elbow and walked in carrying two coffee mugs.

"Thank you! That was a long time to go without a pee break. Did you find any surprises in the motorhome?" I pulled my sweater over my head.

"No, but Bumbles made a beeline out the door, or in his case, I'd call it more of a snail line." Noah smiled and passed me a cup.

I laughed, sat back down on the edge of the bed, and started to take a sip. "Holy crap!" I popped up so quickly I sloshed half the cup of coffee on the floor. "Sorry." I handed the mug back to Noah and jogged to the kitchen for paper towels. After I mopped up the spill, I tossed the towels into the wastebasket by the dresser and scanned the room for my jacket. I didn't recall where I'd left it.

"Would you hold still for a minute?" Noah frowned at me. "You're running around like a crazy person."

"But I gotta go."

"This early on a Sunday morning? Where?"

"Mexico?" It came out more like a question, because I felt so ridiculous breaking it to him.

"Mexico."

"Yeah. Dori and I are driving down there today to her cousins." My tone sounded like we were just heading out for a casual family visit, but I knew he'd know better than that.

"And?"

I expelled a deep breath. "And we hope to find Angela and bring her back up here."

"You're chasing Samuel down to Mexico–just the two of you?"

"Yeah, but we'll let Patrick know what we're doing once we get there. Dori's cousin is going to keep a watch out for Samuel for us, make sure he sticks around if he *does* show up."

"And then you're going to what? Take Angela right out from under his nose? You *are* a crazy person."

"I know it sounds like it, Noah, but Dori believes we can do this, and so do I. I've been on this trajectory since I landed on Samuel's doorstep my first day in Harmony. I have to let it play out."

He looked at me for a long time and set the coffee cups on the nightstand. Wrapping his hand around my arm, he pulled me down on his lap, then he combed my hair off my face with his fingers. "Okay. I get it. You need to do this, but this is serious, dangerous stuff you keep dabbling in, Sydney, and if you're not careful, you could end up with far more than a few bruises."

"I know." I nodded my head. "But this will be it."

"Right." His face was so close I felt the steam of his breath on mine. "You call me. Got it?"

"Got it. Do you mind watching Mr. B and Alice?"

"That's fine. But when you get back, we need to have a talk."

"Sure." I searched his eyes for a clue to what that meant. They revealed nothing. Great.

CHAPTER SIXTEEN

As we crested the last hill before reaching the valley where Dori's cousin told us to meet her, I slowed to a stop, stunned by the scene spread out below. In my rearview mirror was nothing but parched earth; before us were acres and acres of orchards.

"My gosh, look at this place, Dori!" I downshifted and the hatchback carried us toward the Mexican Shangri-La. "How'd they get anything to grow out here?"

"The early Mormons were really good at making something out of nothing. Brigham Young was always ordering them off to some Godforsaken place to create colonies, and they had to figure out a way to survive–fast– because no one was coming to their rescue. He sent them here in the late 1800s when America outlawed polygamy and they started tossing the men in prison."

"It's incredible."

"Yeah. All for the cause." Dori stared through the windshield. "Teresa told me to park at the far end of the last apple orchard. That's where we'd find her."

After entering the compound through an opening in a low stone wall, we turned onto a gravel road that led past three red-roofed stucco houses and a barn. There were no signs of life until we reached the large orchard at the far end of the property, where we saw flashes of children moving between the trees. Stopping the car, we grabbed our jackets from the back seat and stepped into the chilly air.

Walking between the rows, we were met by the curious stares of very young children who were picking apples from the ground and putting them into plastic buckets that were scattered here and there. A few older children with burlap bags slung over their shoulders were atop ladders leaned against the trees. The thick scent of fermented fruit hung in the air, as if the apples had already been turned into cider. In looking at the ones I stepped over, I realized it must have been because they were spotted and deformed.

"There she is." Dori picked up her pace and headed toward a short blonde woman with a baby carrier on her chest and holding the hand of a dark-haired toddler.

"Teresa." Dori leaned over the baby carrier and kissed her cousin's cheek. "I'm happy to see you."

"I'm happy to see you, too." Teresa placed her hand on Dori's arm and studied her face.

"Hi. I'm Sydney." I stepped in beside Dori.

"Nice to meet you." She flicked the bangs off her forehead.

"Who's this little guy?" I looked down at the toddler, who crushed his body into her leg.

"Alejandro. My two-year-old."

"And this must be Isabel." Dori pulled back the fabric on the carrier to reveal the serene face of a sleeping baby with a shock of black hair. "How old is she now?"

"Three-and-a-half-months. She's a really good baby." Teresa smiled down at her daughter then up at Dori. "I've really missed you. How've you been? How's Luke doing?"

As Dori filled her in, I watched the children, who continued to work at their picking. For a group of about two dozen kids it was unnaturally quiet. There was no teasing, fighting, laughing, or running–no schoolyard behavior at all. And even more curious, no school. Why were they out there on a Monday in November instead of sitting behind a classroom desk? And where were the other adults?

When Dori finished she held her palm out to a child dropping an apple into a bucket, echoing my thoughts. "What's all this?"

"What do you mean?" Teresa rocked from side to side as Isabel began to stir.

"I mean, why are you and these children out here picking rotten apples in the cold?" Dori was never one to hold back.

Teresa reddened. "The drought's been really hard on the crops. We're just salvaging what we can."

"But why you, Teresa, why the kids? Where are the men?"

"Gone. Over the border. To work." Her voice rose and Isabel wriggled even more. Teresa rocked harder.

"Your husband, Martin?"

She nodded her head. "And Alex."

"Alex!" Dori put her hand to her throat. "He's what? Eight?"

"Nine."

"My God, Teresa, why?"

"Because there's nothing here, Dori. No money. No jobs. Failed crops." Tears glistened in her eyes. "The elders decided that sending a group to work in the U.S. was our only choice."

"Legally?" Dori put her hands on her hips.

"No."

"What were they thinking? Do you know how dangerous that can be?"

Tears started streaming down Teresa's cheeks and Dori let up. "I'm sorry." She put her arm around her. "Of course you do. Why didn't you tell me all this when I phoned?"

"Couldn't." She shook her head. "They're always checking on me. I took your call in the bathroom and they still could've heard."

"What're you going to do?"

"There's nothing I *can* do."

Watching the too-thin bodies of the children methodically moving from tree to tree, their fingers and cheeks red from the biting air, my heart tightened in my chest. Why was it always the children who suffered? And what kind of callous souls allowed it? That brought Angela to mind and the reason we were there. I felt terrible for Teresa, but if we were going to help Angela we needed to get going. I caught Dori's eyes, hoping she'd understand my signal. She nodded that she had.

"Listen, now that I know the situation, I'm going to figure out some way to get help for you, I promise." Dori ran her hand up and down Teresa's back. "But, we came down here to find Samuel and Angela, and we don't have a lot of time. Have you heard anything?"

"I'm not sure."

"What do you mean?"

"When one of the elders was on the phone a couple days ago, I overheard him mention a town just north of here in New Mexico. It's where the men who smuggled Martin and

Alex live. It could've been Samuel he was talking to. I don't know."

"But no one's actually mentioned Samuel?"

"No."

"How about the other compounds? Do you think he could be there?"

"They're as bad off as we are." Teresa sighed. "If Samuel asked around at all, he'd still be north of the border. We don't just have our own troubles, Dori. We're living in a war zone! That gang you told me that Samuel got involved with is nothing compared to the cartels that rule Northern Mexico. Right now, just a few miles from here, the *Roca* cartel is fighting it out with a smaller cartel for their territory. There are killings and kidnappings every day!"

"That's terrifying! How do you keep you and your kids safe?" Dori reached out and touched the top of Alejandro's head.

"We have some protection from the Mormon colonies that are bigger than us, and there are a few soldiers who patrol the area. Mostly we just hole up and hope they leave us alone."

"What's the name of that town in New Mexico where the smugglers are?"

"Dry Creek."

Dori ran her finger across her bottom lip. "It sounds like hanging around here waiting for Samuel to show up is probably a waste of time."

"Yes, it is. And it's dangerous. I never should've let you come down here. It was wrong of me. I'm sorry. It's just that ..." Her voice caught as she swallowed back a sob. "I'm so scared and alone. I needed to see you. Sometimes I feel like I'd rather be dead."

Dori reached around Teresa's back and hugged her with Isabel wedged between them. "You gotta hang in there."

"I know, but it's *so hard*."

Dori pulled out of the hug and put her hand on Teresa's cheek. "You know I keep my promises, right? I *will* help, somehow. I mean it. But, right now we need to go."

"Yeah. You do." She wiped a tear from the corner of her eye. "And don't stop 'til you get to the border. You two really stick out. You may have been noticed already."

Great. One pursuit by bad guys was enough for any lifetime. We definitely needed to get out of there. I pulled my jacket collar up around my neck and took the car keys out of my pocket.

Dori gently touched her fingertips to Teresa's shoulder. "I'll call really soon."

"Okay." She nodded.

"Love you."

"Love you, too."

"Good to have met you," I said, feeling lame talking to Teresa like we had just run into her at the mall. In actuality she probably spent one day wondering how she was going to make it to the next.

Teresa lifted her hand in good-bye and Dori and I walked back through the orchard. Halfway to the car, I looked over my shoulder at the scene of stolen childhoods. So unfair. And so unforgettable. Definitely not Shangri La.

We managed to make it to the border without incident. There was only one scary moment when a large truck carrying four guys in the back with very big guns passed us going the other way. Dori and I focused our eyes forward and held our breath until they disappeared from the rearview mirror. We hardly said a word to each other until we were back on American soil.

We knew we had reached Dry Creek when we passed the first sprinkling of single-wide trailers. It was yet another sad little high desert town with more than its fair share of faded-blue sky and sandy soil. Knowing there was a chance Samuel would recognize us if we came across him, we decided to stuff our hair into caps and put on sunglasses. Then we slowly cruised up and down the few streets that made up the business district, which in this case was more of an out-of-business district. There was one flat-topped-roof motel with a sign out front that said "V ca cy" that we agreed would make a good hideout. With both our gas tank and stomachs almost on empty, we pulled up to the pumps at the mini mart, which appeared to serve as their only food outlet.

Any thought that we could remain inconspicuous ended the second we walked through the grease-smeared glass doors. The clerk, the man standing at the counter, and a woman grabbing a soda out of a large refrigerator all turned and stared. Walking casually down the nearest aisle and acting completely absorbed in cellophane-wrapped junk food, we pretended not to notice them.

While we paid for our items I evaluated the potential of the clerk to moonlight as a smuggler and couldn't get there. He looked like your average bored minimum-wage worker. He was long over his initial interest in us and didn't even bother with the usual questions for strangers, who probably only pass through when their GPS goes haywire.

Back in the car, Dori asked me to cruise the town one more time and park a safe distance from the motel, but close enough to stake it out. "This place sure doesn't look like any hotbed of smuggling to me," I said to her, driving past a pockmarked stucco house that looked like it was all of six hundred square feet. "There's not even any sign of life around here." I was sick of being in the car and questioning my sanity about agreeing to participate in this escapade. And we still had the drive back.

"A perfect spot, then, right? Off the radar."

"I don't know." I continued down the street and turned left at the next corner. "It was one thing to look for Samuel when he was still in Utah, but here? He could be anywhere."

"Let's just give it a few hours. We've come this far, and we know Teresa's son and husband were smuggled through here."

"Okay. But I'm not staying there tonight." I looked through my driver's side window at the sunbleached blue doors of the motel as we passed by it to find a place to park where we wouldn't be noticed. "I Google-mapped the area and there's a bigger city just a half hour north of here, where we won't have to sleep with bedbugs."

After we ate our way through the minimart food groups—sugar, fat, and carbs—and as the dusk was closing in around us, I recalled the primary reason I'd never be hired as a cop. I couldn't make it through a stakeout without having to pee—several times. And this was one of those times. "I need to use the bathroom." I started to reach for the key in the ignition.

"Wait!" Dori grabbed my arm to stop me. "Look!"

It was Samuel coming out of one of those bleached blue doors. Or, at least it was the physique of Samuel. You couldn't mistake the thick chest and long arms that didn't match his short legs. Although the murky light and the cowboy hat pulled down to his eyes were enough to make us hesitate before declaring a positive I.D. "It's him! It's definitely him!" Dori reached for her door handle. "Call Patrick and look through Samuel's motel room window to see if Angela's in there. Get her out of there quick if she is." Dori kept her eye on Samuel as he walked up the street. "I'm going to follow him."

"But ..."

"I gotta hurry." She opened her door. "Park the car on the next street over. It'll be a safe spot to meet. I'll be back as soon as I see what he's up to."

As I hurried across the street, I phoned Patrick and told him where we were and that we had spotted Samuel. The good news was that with the urgency of the situation there was no time for a lecture as to why Dori and I shouldn't have been there. The bad news was that apprehending Samuel required an interstate arrest warrant; without it no one in New Mexico had the authority to apprehend him. And even though Samuel would likely be charged with endangering Angela's life, along with his numerous other felonies, he probably wouldn't be charged with parental kidnapping if he was her legal guardian. Our taking Angela out of that motel room, however, would definitely be kidnapping. Oh, boy.

Patrick said he'd contact the local authorities and give them a heads up that Samuel was in the area and about his felonious activities in Utah. It was late in the day, though, and getting that arrest warrant was going to take time. When I told him Dori was following Samuel, he was not very happy. He said to call the minute she got back and he'd probably know something by then. No worries there. The sooner we handed the whole mess over to people who actually knew what they were doing, the better.

Looking both directions before approaching Samuel's room, I contemplated the insanity of my new role as a peeping Tom. There was no way I was going to see into that room. The curtains were pulled tight. I put my ear to the door instead and heard the distinctive sound of cartoon character voices blaring from a TV set. Angela had to be in there. What a relief! But according to Patrick, I couldn't do anything about it. Not then.

When Dori popped back into the car and turned around to inspect the back seat, her shoulders drooped and she sighed heavily. "Angela wasn't there?"

"No. She was."

"What! And, you just left her there! I can't believe it! It may have been our only chance!" Her eyes shot darts at me.

"I had to. When I told Patrick about the situation, he said if we took her it'd be kidnapping."

"Well, too bad! We need to help her! I'm going to get her!" She started to open the door.

"No, Dori, listen. Was Samuel headed back to the motel?"

"Yeah, probably."

"While I drive the car to where we can get a better look, you call Patrick and tell him about Samuel's movements. He was going to try and get a hold of someone here to help us. Let's find out what he learned."

Dori cast me a skeptical look, but dialed the phone as I started up the car. In a cool tone, she told Patrick that she had followed Samuel down a side street away from the main highway that led through town, and watched as he talked to a man who had pulled up next to him in a large white van. She left when she thought their discussion was winding down, but she was convinced there was a smuggling deal going down.

Patrick reiterated that the authorities in New Mexico needing an interstate arrest warrant before approaching Samuel, but he added that he was sure he could get one to them the following day. He also gave her a couple of phone numbers and told her that he and they would be on standby if we needed them.

Afraid that Samuel might try to escape across the border, Dori informed Patrick that she and I were going to take shifts watching the motel all night. Before she hung up, she agreed to check in with him every couple of hours.

I pulled the car over to a spot with a good view of the motel, but tucked in behind a large pickup truck. So Cal's little hatchback was going to serve as both our room for the night and our fortress against attack. At least it didn't have bed bugs. I hoped.

When Dori set her phone down, she looked like she was through chewing my head off, but I couldn't be sure. "I still haven't peed." I decided to go way off topic to distract her from her frustration, and because things really were getting desperate in that department. "Do you think I should walk back to the minimart?"

"Better not."

"Well, what do you propose?"

"Just crouch down behind the truck. Do your business there."

"No." She had to be kidding.

"You've never peed on the side of the road?"

"In L.A.? Oh, sure. I have my own little spot right on the Golden State freeway."

"It'll be an adventure."

"Oh, good. That's what I need. Another adventure."

"Just hold it, then." She had no empathy, apparently still miffed.

"Impossible." I stared at her then at the truck in disbelief that I was even contemplating her suggestion. "Okay. Fine." I gave in before my bladder gave out. "I'll pee in the street. But you are never telling a soul about this." I pointed at her. "I mean *never*."

CHAPTER SEVENTEEN

The idea was for one of us to watch out for Samuel while the other one snoozed, but no one was sleeping. We were too on edge. It felt like it had been forever since that first time I laid eyes on Samuel as he stood glowering down on me in his front yard. It also felt like from that first moment, I knew *this* moment would come. Within the security of my Southern California life, I never had to confront evil. It stayed a safe distance away on the pages of the newspaper or images on a screen. With Samuel, however, the distance between evil and myself was the width of an eyelash. It was not a concept, but a terrifying tangible thing. Still, it would have been easy to ignore. Just turn my back. Go on with my life. No one expected me to involve myself in *this* war with *this* devil. Except for her. I looked over at Dori, her shoulder almost touching mine as she tugged on the sleeves of her jacket to cover her hands. It was getting colder by the minute in our thin shelter.

As cold as it was, though, the camaraderie I felt with Dori, encased in our metal shelter, put me in the mood to ponder the big questions about what makes the universe and people tick. "Do you think it's possible for someone to be pure evil, without any chance to change whatsoever?" I asked softly.

She turned toward me. "Our leaders taught us that you on the outside are evil and you live in Hell–actual physical Hell. The first time I recall my mom taking me to a store, I spent the whole time hiding in her skirts, waiting for someone to snatch me away or devour live puppies or something. Ha! I was so scared, but nothing happened. Instead, people smiled and said how cute I was, or mostly just went about their business. They were nice. Even at that age, I knew something wasn't right about what we were told. Maybe it was because they hadn't had enough time to brainwash me. When my father showed up, mostly to get my mother pregnant, he was anything *but nice*. I was so afraid of him." She hesitated, her thoughts turned inward. "My father's a cruel man and, no, I don't think he's capable of change. Not in this lifetime. What I do think is the polygamist cult leaders are infected with a mental illness they pass on to their wives and children. The only way to prevent their sickness from spreading is to put them in prison and throw away the key. If they're not evil; they're close."

Listening to the powerful simplicity in the way Dori formed her convictions was impressive. "Where do you get your strength? What makes you different from women like Teresa? Why didn't they see what you saw?"

"I'm not special. I was lucky, really, that they kicked me and Luke out. With most of the women, they're married with two kids before they realize what's really happening, then they're in so deep they don't know what to do. Add to that the abuse and brainwashing they're subjected to every waking moment of their lives, and they don't stand a chance. That's why they need *us*."

"But, you *are special*, Dori. You're an incredibly clear thinker. That's rare. And it's a privilege to know you."

The look on her face said she hadn't heard those kinds of words very often in her young life. "Thank you."

"I was clueless at your age."

"But you're not now." She shrugged.

"No. I suppose not. But did I need nutjob felons to show me the path to enlightenment? Really?" I glanced through the window at the dim motel light outside Samuel's room.

"But look at all the fun you're having."

"Right." I hugged my torso and shifted, trying to shake my numb legs back to life.

We checked in twice with Patrick to tell him that nothing was going on, and I was finally succumbing to sleep when Dori whispered, "There's the van!"

It was two o'clock. We called Patrick right away. He picked up on the first ring and said he'd put the local agencies on alert. He also said that he'd call right back and stay on the line with us so he'd know what was happening.

The van approached from the side of the motel away from the little office and stopped well back of the entrance to the parking lot, immediately cutting its lights. The door to Samuel's room opened and a few seconds passed before he appeared carrying a duffle bag over his shoulder and Angela in his arms. She had her head on his chest like she was asleep. Samuel hurried to the van and disappeared through a side door that the driver had slid open. The second the door closed the van pulled away.

"Follow him, but wait 'til he's a ways down the street, and make sure your lights are off." Dori's nose was practically touching the windshield.

"I won't be able to see the road."

"Just follow his lights, but stay back."

Keeping my eyes focused ahead, thankful that the town had rolled up the sidewalks for the night and there was not another person out, I accelerated to keep the van in my sights. He was moving pretty fast, and I prayed that the night critters roaming the desert would see me coming before committing hari-kiri by hatchback. After several miles, the van took a sharp left into the open range down a narrow sandy path. "See if you can bring up the GPS on your phone, so you can tell Patrick where we are." The car bumped so hard every time I strayed from the path and over bushes that my hair touched the headliner. "I wish he'd hurry up and call."

"The GPS isn't going to do us any good." Dori held her phone down by her legs and had her hand cupped over it to keep it from shining any light into the car. "There aren't any identifying markers showing up. We're going to have to keep track of where we are ourselves. Do you know what direction we're headed?"

"I know we're going south, because when we started following him we were on the road we took from the border. Let me think about it." I drummed my fingers on the steering wheel. "He veered left, so that means we're headed east. Southeast."

"Good."

"Yeah, except what're we going to do if the Border Patrol or whoever is supposed to help us doesn't show up? And why hasn't Patrick called!"

"No cell service." She clicked the phone to sleep mode and straightened up.

"Great! Now, what?" We jostled along, the knot in my stomach getting tighter by the second.

"We keep following them."

"To do what? We can't stop them from taking Angela over the border. They probably have weapons."

"Maybe the cell service will come back up."

"It's not gonna to happen, Dori. The best chance to help Angela is for us to head back to where there *is* cell service and give Patrick the most accurate description of their location we can."

"You're right." She sighed. "But we gotta hurry or they'll be long gone by the time help arrives."

"I'll try, but I can only go so fast without lights and we need to leave them off 'til we're out of range of their rearview mirrors."

As I started into a U-turn, suddenly the whole world lit up like it was high noon. "Shit! What's going on?"

"Stop!" Dori rolled her window down and we both stared through it, our eyes adjusting to the brightness. The quiet night succumbed to a cacophony of shouts, loud motors, and what sounded like gunshots.

Framed by the lights, a blur of bodies darted in every direction, chased by uniformed officers. Out of the commotion emerged Samuel, heading straight for us. Running hard, the officer pursuing him trained a flashlight on his back, but he wasn't closing the twenty-yard gap. When Samuel finally spotted our car, he peeled off his course without losing speed. "Hang on!" I flipped on my lights and accelerated after him straight over bush after bush. It slowed us down a bit, but the faithful hatchback was still faster than Samuel. Right on his heels, I blared my horn at his back, but he wouldn't stop. "Should I run the bastard down?" My adrenalin pumped so hard that my pent-up scorn for him wanted to see him in pieces all over the desert.

"Probably not." Dori sounded like she had entertained the notion also, but reason won out. "Let's just keep on him. Try to herd him back toward the officers."

Making an arc, I came at Samuel from the side, forcing him to change direction. I repeated the maneuver every time he headed for open desert. His lungs and legs finally started to give out as he slowed to a jog. Flipping my brights on and off, easing the car along, I was so close I could have tapped his legs. He never turned around. Did he think we were going away? Arrogant to the end.

Over my left shoulder I noticed the officer, now with a gun in his hand as well as a flashlight. Keeping pace with us, when he knew he had my attention he motioned for me to stop. Complying, we watched as he moved closer to Samuel. "Halt and put your hands up, now!" he ordered.

When Samuel ignored him, another officer approached from the other side of the car. "You're surrounded. Put your hands in the air!" He trained his gun on him.

Finally stopping and breathing hard, Samuel bent forward with his hands on his knees, the officers' eyes and guns focused on him. He then slowly stood up and raised his arms.

When the officers were through frisking Samuel, I got out of the car and moved to stand by Dori. We wanted to be in his path when they walked by us. We wanted to see his eyes when he recognized us. We wanted Samuel to know that, yes, we would have tracked him to the ends of the earth to see him put away forever for what he did to the women and children in his life. And we got what we wanted. The reflection of confusion then recognition then anger that crossed his face was as sweet a victory as we had ever tasted.

I navigated the car back through the brush and over to the crowd of vehicles and people illuminated by headlamps and flashlights. There were several dark-haired men and women seated on the ground. An officer with a rifle in his hands stood watch over them. Another officer was frisking a man leaned against a white Border Patrol SUV with his arms stretched above him and his legs spread apart. He had to be the smuggler.

Feeling totally out of our element–I wonder why–but anxious to check on Angela, we hung by our car until an officer with *US Marshal* printed across his bulletproof vest, standing at the open door of the van, noticed us. We hurried over. "Is there a little girl in there?" Dori asked, looking past him trying to see into the van. His crossed arms and bulky build barred the view. "I'm Dori Hunt, and this is my friend, Sydney. We're the ones who called Deputy Crane in Utah about Samuel Vaullie and followed the van here," she added when the officer didn't answer right away.

"I guessed that. I didn't figure you were out for a late-night drive." His stern expression relaxed a bit.

"Angela, the little girl, is my cousin."

Cousin? Were there any Harmony polygamists Dori *wasn't* related to?

"Is she in there?" she asked again. "She's probably really frightened."

"Yes. With another marshal."

"Thank, God!" She grabbed my wrist and I felt the shaking in her hand.

"Is she all right? Can I go in?"

The officer turned and leaned his head into the van. When he straightened up, he stepped aside. "Go ahead."

Dori hung onto the door handle and pulled herself up. I stayed behind, not wanting to overwhelm Angela.

"I thought it was only Samuel and Angela in the van with the driver. Where did all these other people come from?" I asked the marshal, who resumed his post at the van door. I looked at the men and women on the ground. Most were resting their heads on their bent knees. Samuel sat with his back against the tire of one of the SUVs, his hands handcuffed behind his back.

"A lot of smugglers work both ends–drop off and pick up–illegal immigration to go."

"What happens to them?"

"The smugglers, we arrest. The rest of them mostly just get booted back across the border."

"What'll you do with Samuel?"

"He'll be put in jail here 'til it's all sorted out."

"Good. I plan on having front row seats for his trial." I pulled my jacket tighter around me and stamped my feet to try and warm up. It wasn't working. "You think they'll let Dori take Angela with us?"

"No. That'll either be handled by our office or the D.A.'s investigative team from your area." He evened his weight out between his legs and crossed his arms again.

Oh, boy. Dori wasn't going to be happy about that one. "Won't that be hard on Angela?"

"They know what they're doing." He turned around when he heard movement behind him. It was Dori and a woman marshal at the van door with Angela wedged between them. Her hair had pulled loose from her braid and was plumed out like feathers against her thin cheeks. The dark crescents under her frightened eyes stood out against her white skin, but she still managed a soft smile when she noticed me. I wriggled my fingers at her and smiled back.

Dori stepped down from the van and reached up to lift Angela to the ground, then the marshal stepped down beside them. Bending down so that her nose was almost touching Angela's and using her body to block her from seeing Samuel, Dori wrapped her hands around her shoulders. "Marshal Pam is going to drive you to her office, Angela, and Sydney and I are going to follow right behind you."

"No! I want you to stay with me!" Angela gripped at Dori's jacket, her tone high and pleading.

I glanced over at Samuel to see if the sound of Angela's heartbreaking voice would have any effect on him. He didn't even look over.

"We'll be with you, *the whole ride*. You'll be able to see our lights right behind you, right, Marshal Pam?"

"That's right. You'll be able to watch them from the back seat." Marshal Pam held her open palm out to Angela. "It's time to go now, honey."

Dori released Angela and stood up. "Go on now, love. The sooner we get to Marshal Pam's office, the sooner you get to go home."

"But ..." She leaned her head to look past us for her father, but Dori continued to block her view. When she stared up at Dori, her eyes filled with tears.

"It's going to be all right, I promise." Dori knelt and pulled her into an embrace.

Before we left to follow them, Marshal Pam gave us the location of her office. It was in the city where I had told Dori I wanted to spend the night–before we were caught up in the stakeout of Samuel. On the ride, Dori said that it was her intention to stay with Angela until she was safe in Harmony–which meant I was staying too. At least we were going to end up in that motel I had researched, rather than the fleabag one in Dry Creek. Dori was hopeful it would only be for a night or two more. It had better be–I was already testing the limits of Noah's good nature in leaving him to take care of Mr. B and Alice–let alone his desire for us to have a *little chat*.

CHAPTER EIGHTEEN

Dori and I stood at the door of Samuel Vaullie's house with Angela between us. Marshal Pam had brought her there to release her to Helen, which wasn't our choice by any means. On the drive back to Harmony from New Mexico, the two of us had a long time to discuss Angela's custody arrangements. We were determined that if there was any way to remove her from that toxic environment we were going to find it.

One question I finally had answered on our ride was that even Dori had no idea exactly who Angela's mother was. I had assumed from the beginning it was Helen, but Dori explained that oftentimes in polygamist cults the leaders mandate that children and mothers be separated. That a mother could be coerced to give up her own child was strong evidence of the leaders' expertise at brainwashing.

As Marshal Pam explained the process, Helen's clenched jaw signaled that even though she didn't look over she was highly aware of Dori's eyes boring into her. After the marshal finished speaking, she stepped back and Helen opened her arms to Angela in a weak attempt to play the loving guardian of the innocent. Pressing herself tightly into Dori's side, Angela was having no part of it.

"Come along now, Angela." Helen's voice took on a phony singsong tone; one I had never heard her use. "Agnes needs your help in making chocolate chip cookies, your favorite."

Angela buried her face deeper into Dori's legs.

Helen reached out and touched Angela's back. "Everyone's waiting to see you."

"I don't wanna see them! I wanna go with Dori!" Angela turned her head to look at Helen and twisted her shoulders as if to rid herself of her touch.

"Dori needs to go home now, don't you, Dori." Helen turned the corners of her mouth up, struggling to hide her vexation from the marshal, but her expression was more of a grimace than a smile.

Dori pulled back from Angela and knelt down. "Lucas is waiting for me, so I do need to go." She smoothed the hair back from Angela's face. "But I'll be back tomorrow." She looked up pointedly at Helen.

"In the morning? I want you to come in the morning."

"I'll come as soon as I can."

"Will you bring Ruthie? You told me I could see Ruthie when we got back."

"Sure. I'll ask her to come along."

"And her baby. I wanna see her baby." Angela gripped Dori's arm.

"Okay. But right now you need to go inside and help Agnes with the cookies. You can give one to Ruthie tomorrow, how 'bout that? I'll bet they're her favorite too."

"I'll make a big one for her." Angela smiled for the first time and let go of Dori's arm.

Dori drew Angela to her in a tight hug. "I'll be back before you know it."

When Dori and I walked into Dusty's, it felt pretty lively for a fall evening. The tables were almost filled. The new waitress Dusty hired was hustling between them, and there were no seats left at the counter. We expected Luke to be working the tables also, but he was seated at the counter instead. Dori marched over like she was going to pounce on him for dereliction of duty. Before she could open her mouth the man sitting next to Luke at the counter turned to say something to him and we both stood in shock.

"Malachi?" Dori got the question out first.

He looked over and a smile lit up his eyes.

Before she could put up her normal guard, she flushed from her neck to her cheeks, the first time I'd ever seen her do so, her eyes as bright as his. Embarrassed at her own reaction, she recovered quickly by burying her pleasure at seeing him in concern. "What're you doing here?"

"I heard the food's good." He was still smiling.

"What?"

"And we're celebrating." He held up a half empty dish of ice cream and nodded at the one in front of Luke.

"You are?"

"Yeah, Deputy Crane solved the Bliss Mine cold case!" Luke swiveled toward Patrick, who was seated on the other side of him.

"Couldn't have done it without Luke's help." Patrick patted Luke's back, and Luke didn't flinch–a first for him too. "DNA evidence from both the victim and his killer were on the fabric he found in the mine."

"Yeah, and the killer's in one of the mug books!"

"Is he still alive?"

"Nah." Luke shook his head. "Died in prison for another murder, right, Deputy Crane?" Luke reached behind him, picked up his ice cream bowl and dug his spoon into it.

"Yeah. In 2010."

"Amazing." I spoke up. "Does the family of the victim know?"

"They do. It was tough on them having to relive the murder, but they appreciated the closure."

"That's wonderful. I can see why you're celebrating. We may have to join in, right, Dori?" I tugged at her elbow to get her attention. She was still standing there, speechless. "You wanna join us at a booth?" I asked the men.

"I've only got a few minutes before I need to get back to the office, but okay." Patrick picked up his ice cream bowl and coffee cup and stood up.

"To be sure." Malachi stood also.

"Luke, you coming?" I asked, when he just kept on eating.

"I think he'd better get back to work." Dori glanced at the pile of dishes in a tub at the end of the counter.

"Yes. I need to get back to work." Luke scraped the last of his ice cream from the bowl and slid off his chair, on to the next thing.

When we settled into the booth, Patrick and Malachi across from us, the waitress came over and Dori and I ordered dinner. We hadn't eaten much all day and were famished. It was so bizarre to see Malachi Keane, Irish balladeer and secret agent–hanging out in a booth at Dusty's. In Harmony, Utah! Dori must have been thinking the same thing, staring at him from underneath her eyelashes, while Patrick began filling us in on the case against the Midgeman brothers.

He told us Reed was still in the hospital, but expected to make a complete recovery from his gunshot wounds, and Seth was in jail and had already had his preliminary hearing. The Bailey boys, however, were out on bail. Of course, Genevieve would work her will to keep them with her as long as she could. With the counts against them, will or not, her view of them for at least a few years was going to be through a locked cell. I hoped.

Patrick had been updated on our adventure on the border by the agencies in New Mexico. With our interest in Angela's living situation heavy on our minds, Dori was anxious to find out if he had any ideas about how we could get her out of Samuel's compound. "We just had to watch the marshal hand Angela over to Helen. If she stays there, God knows what will happen to her. Can you think of anything we can do? We're not even sure Helen is her mother."

"She's not."

"How do you know that?" Dori sat up straight.

"Angela's mother committed suicide shortly after she was born."

"And you're just now telling us this?"

"I just found out myself."

"How?"

"When I was helping with the paperwork to get Angela back here, I discovered her mother's death certificate."

"Wow. This changes everything." I could almost hear the wheels spinning in Dori's brain. "So, no one except Samuel has official custody of Angela?"

"No."

"Then, why did she have to go back there?"

"I'm sure the agencies determined it would be best since it's her home and Helen and Samuel's other wives and children are her family."

"Well, so am I. And so is Ruthie." Dori looked over at me. I could tell she had already hatched a plan. I just hoped it didn't involve kidnapping. "Can I get a copy of that death certificate?"

"It's public record." Patrick tugged his wallet from his pocket and pulled out a few bills. "Come by the office tomorrow morning and we'll talk." Patrick was a small-town deputy, but he was a really smart guy. He'd help Angela if he could, but he'd also make sure things were handled the right way. "I gotta get back to the office." He set the bills on the table. "Malachi, nice meeting you. Ladies." He tipped his head at us.

"See you in the morning." Dori raised her hand at him then turned her full attention on Malachi. "So?"

"Yes?"

"Why are you here?"

"Just passin' through."

"Impossible. Harmony's not on the way from or to *anywhere.*"

"That's right. No one lands here, except by taking a wrong turn." I joined in. It had been a tiring few days and from the smile that had returned to her eyes Dori may not have minded a long verbal dance with Malachi, but I was missing my dog and cat, not to mention Noah, and I wanted to get back to my tiny home. I was also more than a little concerned that Malachi's appearance may have a direct connection to a cartel's interest in permanently eliminating me from the planet. "You don't take wrong turns, Malachi. Why are you in Utah?"

He lowered his voice. "I've been in Salt Lake City. We had reason to believe the Rock cartel had moved into the area."

"And had they?" I could already feel my adrenaline kicking in on that news.

"Yes."

"Oh, boy."

"But we haven't found any evidence they're doing business anywhere else in the state yet."

"Yet? That's a real confidence booster."

"Like a lot of long-dead cartels, they think they're gonna rule the drug and trafficking world, but 'tain't gonna happen. They're heavily involved in battling it out with at least two other cartels in Mexico. Carrick didn't have a clue what he was taking on with those gangs. For him, murder is a part of doing business. For them, it's pure sport. They enjoy every second of it."

"Wait." A cold chill bumped down my spine. "Is this battle you're referring to happening in Chihuahua?"

"Uh, huh."

"My God, Dori, didn't Teresa mention a Roca cartel in their area?"

"Yeah, and?"

"Roca. Rock. Carrick's cartel has to be the one she was talking about. Right?"

"That's the one." Malachi answered.

"We were right there."

"I know." He narrowed his eyes at us.

"So, your showing up here is not just about Salt Lake City."

"Ya got that right. It's about you two making very bad choices about where to holiday."

"It was about our helping Angela." Dori crossed her arms.

"Do you think Dori's cousin and her family could be in danger?" I asked.

"No more than they are already just by living where they do."

"Should we be worried?" I was back to feeling as vulnerable as I felt in New York.

"You should be aware. And, really, don't you think it's about time you find day jobs that don't involve shootouts and chasing down smugglers?"

"You heard about the Bliss Mine, huh?"

"Oh, yeah. Deputy Crane told ..." He was cut off mid-sentence.

"So, you're back!" It was Genevieve clicking her way on spike-heeled boots straight toward our booth. "Don't think I'm not considering suing you for what you did to Floyd and Lloyd!" She put her hand on the seat behind Malachi and glared down at us.

"You mean, save their lives?" Dori glared back at her.

"You did no such thing. They told me all about it. The cut on Lloyd's cheek may leave a permanent scar."

"Maybe it'll give him some character. He's not getting it anywhere else." I cut in.

"You've had it out for them ever since you landed in this town." She turned on me. "They could've been killed! And now they have to be put through the emotional distress of a trial!"

"Yeah. By their own doing. They were stealing for a metal theft gang. And they kidnapped an old man. What part of that don't you understand?"

"Those men forced them into it!"

"No! They're punks and thieves, through and through!"

Taking a deep breath before launching into another attack on me, Genevieve's eyes drifted down, and she finally noticed Malachi. After a split-second assessment of his looks and potential as fresh meat, she suddenly forgot her long-suffering sons and her entire demeanor changed. "We'll take this up later." She dismissed me and stepped around so she was facing Malachi. "I'm Genevieve Bailey." She held out her hand. "I don't believe we've met."

He shook it lightly. "Malachi Keene."

When Genevieve heard his trace of an accent, the deal was sealed. She wanted him. You could almost see her flesh quiver. "Oh! You're from England! We never get any foreign visitors around here. You must let me join you!" She bent down, preparing to squeeze her pudgy butt in next to him.

Malachi looked over at Dori for help, at a loss for what to do.

The corner of Dori's mouth turned up. I could tell she was having a hard time holding back a laugh.

Then I felt a hand on my shoulder and looked up into Noah's eyes. They weren't smiling.

"Noah!" Genevieve gushed. "We have a visitor from England!" She ran her sharp fingernails along Malachi's shoulder. "Come join us!"

Oh, so suddenly Genevieve was throwing a party?

Malachi made no move whatsoever to let her sit down.

"Ireland." Noah said to Genevieve. "We've met."

"*You have*?" I asked. I was so confused.

"Yup."

"When?"

"Earlier."

"Ireland! Even better. I've always wanted to go there! Kiss the Blarney stone and all that. Sit down with us!" Genevieve was still bent over, ready to move in next to Malachi. Add Noah to the equation, and she'd be the filling to the man sandwich of her orgasmic dreams. Only Malachi hadn't moved an inch.

"Can't. We're leaving." Noah told her, still staring at me.

"But my dinner?" No one else could hear it over the crazy turn the conversation had taken, but my stomach was growling.

"I'll tell Dusty to box it up." Noah turned and walked over to the counter.

Whoa. Okay? I'd never known Noah to be rude, but he hadn't even said hello to anyone. I shrugged my shoulders at Dori with a questioning look. She shook her head, no help.

"We got to be leavin' too." Malachi reached his hand across the table and set it on top of Dori's.

It was her turn to glance over at me, also confused at the turn of events.

"I'll have your dinner packed." He picked Genevieve's hand off his shoulder like it was a spider come to rest and moved out of the booth.

Genevieve was forced to step back. Looking from Malachi to Dori and back again, her expression was far more bewildered than Dori's and mine.

"A pleasure to meet you, Genevieve." Malachi picked up her hand and gently kissed the back of it then glanced at Dori and winked.

"Uh, oh ..." Genevieve had no reply.

Dori and I shrugged our shoulders once again and slid out of the booth.

CHAPTER NINETEEN

Noah sat down across from me at the motorhome's dinette. I was finally digging into my dinner after feeding Mr. B and Alice. They had been very happy to see me, well, at least Mr. B was. With Alice you could never tell. He was stretched out at my feet. Shoeless, I ran my sock-covered foot along his lengthy flank. I needed the reassurance of his soft warm fur and the gentle rise and fall of his breathing. Noah hadn't said two words to me as he guided me to my car then got into his truck to follow me back to the ranch, or as I put away my suitcase and reheated my dinner. Something was coming and it couldn't be good.

"You sure you don't want some of this?" I cleared my throat, unable to look right at him. As hungry as I had been, the food had lost its appeal.

"No. I'm good."

I poked at the limp green beans. If he had something to say, I sure wished he'd get to it. The suspense was making me crazy. "So, how was your week?" I ventured.

"The usual. And, yours?"

What? He obviously had heard what my week had been like. Was that a trick question?

"How's the weather on the Mexican border this time of year?" He leaned back against the seat, crossed his arms, and stared evenly at me.

The weather? He was asking about the weather? I squirmed under his gaze. Noah wasn't the type to play a cat and mouse game and neither was I. "Okay, let's hear it." I pushed my plate to the side.

"What's that?"

"You're obviously angry."

"Curious is more like it."

"Okay? Can you be a little more specific?"

"Sure. I was just wondering why you choose to live without ties to anyone or anything other than your cat and dog?"

Whoa! I felt like I'd been beaned upside the head with a tire iron. What in the hell was he talking about? "What are you insinuating?" I could barely get the words out with my jaw already beginning to shake. He may have only been curious, but I was irate.

"You have no attachments."

"Excuse me? I just drove all the way to Mexico and back because of my attachment to Angela."

"Are you sure?"

"Of course, I'm sure!" I pressed my palms into the table in front of me and leaned toward him. "She'd been kidnapped by her insane father! We needed to get her back."

"That's responsibility. Not attachment." His voice was soft and calm, which riled me even more.

"Oh my, God! What's the difference?"

"Responsibility comes from obligation. Once the obligation's met, you're free to move on. Attachments are permanent bonds."

"Wow! So basically what you're accusing me of is having no bonds except to my pets. That's ridiculous! I have my girlfriends back home, and Harry, and my family in New York, Dori." I counted them off on my fingers.

"Except for Dori, those are just names on your Christmas card list, and if your recent actions are any indication, soon Dori will be too."

"I don't send Christmas cards. And what do you mean by my *recent actions*?"

"Your ties only reach as far as your wave good-bye."

"That's just not true."

"Really? So why didn't I hear from you the past few days? He picked up his hat from the seat next to him and started to put it on his head. "No need to answer. You just did when you ticked off that list of yours."

Shit! He wasn't on the list. My resentment was immediately displaced by regret. "Wait! Don't go!" I put my hand on his forearm. "Can't we talk this out?"

"Where's that gonna get us? Do you even know what you want?"

"I ..." I hesitated. What did I want? The only thing I was sure of was I didn't want him to walk out the door.

"I didn't think so." He started to scoot off the booth.

"No." I pressed my fingers even tighter into his arm. "Please. Just give me a minute. I'm not good at this."

Noah settled back into the seat, but kept his hand on his hat.

"Look. I know you think I'm incapable of forming deep ties to anything, but you're wrong. I didn't grow up in a huge family, but I was really close to my mom and dad and grandmother. I miss them terribly, every day." Oh, boy. I already felt myself starting to tear up, and that wasn't helpful. I steered it in another direction. "I spent my whole life in L.A.

How could I help but be attached to it? But I also needed out of there. I was tired of life happening *to me*. I wanted to take more control."

"And the last couple of months are what you call being in control?"

"Yes. No. I mean it started out that way. Things just didn't work out in New York."

"Ya think?"

"And then, you know, I got caught up in the whole Samuel thing with Dori. But, that's over now, and ..."

"Yeah?"

"And now I need to figure out what I wanna do next."

"An easy decision, because you have no attachments, no one else who has to figure into your plans."

"Oh, that was clever." I frowned at him. "You didn't tell me you were on your high school debate team."

"Not clever. Just letting you know I get it. You think you're totally independent. Only in all that freedom you're carving out for yourself, you may want to consider the fallout from complete self-reliance. When you involve yourself in people's lives, or when you sleep with someone for more than a one-night-stand, they think you care. It's dishonest and thoughtless to form relationships and toss them away. People aren't disposable. And they don't like to be treated that way. So, good luck with that." He picked up his hat again and set it on his head.

I was stunned and speechless. It was the harshest thing anyone had ever said to me. And the second time in just a few months that a man had called me out for dishonesty. Was I lying to myself and everyone else? With Harry, I had let months go by without telling him that I planned to leave. With

Noah, I moved into his bed, but hadn't had the guts to admit that he had moved into my heart–to him or to myself. Looking at those eyes that attracted me from the first time they twinkled at me, but now had gone cold, I felt sick with the thought of never seeing them again. But that was exactly what was going to happen if I didn't keep him from walking out the door. If I did stop him, however, I'd be making a long unscheduled stay right there in Harmony, Utah. Harmony, Utah? Aye, yai, yai.

He moved from the seat and stood up.

"Okay. Okay. I get it. I'm sorry. I should have called you from the road and let you know what was going on."

Not responding, he stared down at me–his eyes still cold– and put his hat on his head. Clearly, a simple apology wasn't enough to mend what I had broken.

Standing up also and stepping so close to him that the brim of his hat almost touched my forehead, I forced myself to lock onto his hard stare. I wanted him to recognize the truth in my eyes and the sincerity of my words. "You're wrong to say I don't care," I sighed. "I've been hiding behind emotional walls because I can't conceive of having fallen in love with this place. Look at it!" I pointed at the blinds covering the view to a cold and parched high desert landscape. "It's, it's so ... dusty!"

The corner of Noah's mouth turned up, but only for a split second before he set his jaw again.

"And you!" I tapped his chest with my forefinger. "Did you have to be so sexy cowboyie? I mean, like right out of some 1940s Western? Jeez. And you're so steady. And thoughtful! Yeah, thoughtful! How was I supposed to keep from falling in love with that? You tell me that!"

The light was back in his eyes as he crossed his arms. "Cowboyie?"

"Yeah, cowboyie!" I smiled. I couldn't help it. It sounded pretty ridiculous.

Despite the softening of his look, Noah just stood there. Shoot! It was pretty clear I had just declared that I loved him. And he was giving me no clues as to how he felt about that. Not good.

"Does that mean I earned a phone call?"

We were back to that? "Yeah."

"Every night before bed, when you're out chasing felons?" He finally smiled.

"I'm not going to be chasing any more felons."

"Right."

"I'm not ..." I started to protest.

He took off his hat, closed the small space between us and buried my answer in his kiss. Sliding his arms around my back, he pressed so hard into me it took my breath away, but who needed air?

When he finally pulled back, I whispered, "You did hear the whole part about falling in love with you?"

"Uh, huh."

"And?" It had been in the heat of the moment, but I had said it and despite the kiss I was insecure enough to want him to say he felt the same way.

"And how was I supposed to keep from falling in love with all that red hair and fieriness."

"Fieriness?"

"Yeah." He brushed the hair back from my face and kissed my temple, the back of my ear then my neck, and I was gone. Toast.

CHAPTER TWENTY

There we were again, a rather peculiar league of women, Dori, V.A., Ruthie, and me, standing on Samuel's doorstep waiting for someone to answer our knock. The game plan was to convince Helen to hand Angela over to us so she could live with Ruthie at Miriam's until further notice—or forever, if things went really well. We weren't expecting that.

Dori's defense was a copy of Angela's mother's death certificate, which she gripped in her hand. She had acquired it from Patrick, along with advice on how to handle the negotiation. Something like, "Be nice. It'll get you further and keep you out of court. You don't want a custody battle. It would be wrong to put Angela through it, and there's a very good chance you'd lose."

We had shown up very early, suspicious that Helen might try to hide Angela in another home in the compound, since Dori told her we would be coming. When Agnes finally answered the door, Angela was right there beside her, still dressed in her pajamas.

"Ruthie!" Angela threw herself at Ruthie's legs, hugging them tight. "Where's your baby?" She looked up at her.

"Back home with Miriam." Ruthie's eyes glistened as she ran her hand over Angela's soft blonde hair.

"But I wanna see her."

"You will."

"Is Helen around?" Dori asked Agnes.

"Um. She hasn't come down yet." Agnes cast unsure eyes over her shoulder.

"We'll wait in the kitchen." V.A. put her foot on the threshold, not allowing for any protest. "Angela, how 'bout if Ruthie takes you up to your room so you can get dressed." V.A. caught Ruthie's eyes and mouthed, "Keep her there."

"Come on, sweetheart." Ruthie reached for Angela's hand.

"Father Samuel took me way far away." Angela said, as Ruthie led her inside. "I was in a cave."

"You were?" Ruthie kept her tone light. "I'd like to hear about that."

The four of us had talked on the drive over that it was going to take some time for Angela to recover from the emotional trauma she had suffered at the hands of Samuel. Ruthie told us she was sure she could help her. It was remarkable to witness how strong Ruthie had become when she was finally out of the reach of Samuel–a testimony to the resilience of the human spirit. I prayed Angela would be just as resilient. She was young. There was that. And if it seemed like she needed outside support, we agreed we'd find it. But first we had to get her out of the dim dungeon they called home.

Walking down the hall to the kitchen I took in how truly dismal the place was. Thin cracks ran from the doors and window frames over walls covered in faded and peeling paint; dim lights cast a yellowish tint on everything; and there was not one personal item anywhere. No photographs. No schoolwork affixed to the refrigerator by magnets collected on family vacations. How could they stand living there? I looked at Agnes as she nervously hovered in the doorway while Dori, V.A. and I took seats around the kitchen table.

"I'll go get Helen." She started to dart back down the hall and ran smack into her. "Oh, sorry," we heard her say over her retreating footsteps. "I need to use the bathroom." A mouse of a woman, she must have decided she wanted no part of what she feared would be coming next.

"You're here early." Helen crossed her arms, taking in the three of us.

"We're concerned about Angela and wanted to talk with you about it. Won't you sit down?" Dori set her hand on the seat of the empty chair next to her.

Helen pulled it out and perched on the edge of it, then re-crossed her arms. "We're all concerned about Angela."

"Good." Dori nodded her head. "Samuel put her through a lot."

"And for that and all the other crimes he committed, he's gonna end up in prison 'til he's an old man or dead." V.A. spoke up. "He'll never be part of Angela's life again."

"So, there's the matter of what's going to be best for Angela with Samuel out of the picture," Dori said.

"What's best for Angela is that she remain here with us." Helen looked from one to the other of us, her jaw tight. Dori's soft tone had done nothing to dispel Helen's suspicion about why we were there. She knew exactly what we wanted and she was going to do everything in her power to see we didn't get it.

I could tell from Dori's rigid body language in reaction to Helen's statement that she was already thinking about abandoning Patrick's advice. Not good. "Angela seems to be the happiest with Ruthie," I said to Helen before Dori could speak.

"And Ruthie would still be here if you all hadn't stuck your noses in where they didn't belong."

"Ruthie'd be dead if we hadn't stuck our noses in." V.A. glared at Helen.

"But we're here about Angela," I said, trying to keep the conversation calm and on track. "And about making sure the place she lives is a nurturing environment that will help her recover from her trauma."

"Who are you to say we're not nurturing? And, *who are you* in all this anyway?" Helen practically spat at me. So much for keeping things calm.

"Helen." Dori waited to speak until Helen looked over at her. "We're not here to judge you for what you did or did not do for Angela in the past. We're here to talk about her future. And she has none here. She's a smart, loving little girl, who deserves a life outside these walls. She can't get that unless you let her leave."

"I'm her mother." There was a slight crack in Helen's guard. I could see it as she turned her head away.

Dori saw it too. "No. You're not, Helen."

"What do you mean?" She snapped her head around.

"Her mother's dead."

"Stepmother, then."

"Not that, either." Dori shook her head.

"Let Angela go, Helen." V.A. stretched her hand across the table and patted Helen's forearm that was still tightly wound around her torso. Helen flinched, but didn't pull her arm away as V.A. continued, "Miriam and Odelia want Angela to live with them and Ruthie and Remy. They'll give her a chance at a good life, Helen. See that she goes to school. You know it's the right thing to do."

Helen stared through the window above the kitchen sink for a long time, then without looking at them, she finally said, "All right. Take her."

Really? Just like that? I stared at Helen, wondering why she caved so easily. Was it because she thought she'd lose the war? Or, was it because in the end she really didn't care whether Angela stayed or went. She wasn't her child, after all. Had Helen spent so much of her life without kindness and love that she'd lost the ability to mourn Angela's leaving?

Sad, but not our problem anymore. Angela was going home with Ruthie, who couldn't pack her up fast enough. On the ride to Miriam's the little hatchback had never been so full of passengers—or hope.

Angela's blithe spirit danced all the way to the porch when she saw Miriam waiting for them with Remy in her arms. It wasn't going to be all lollipops and sunshine while she adjusted to her new life, and somewhere along the way the custody details would have to be worked out. But Angela would grow up surrounded by strong women with big hearts—a very good start.

After leaving V.A., Ruthie, and Angela at the ranch, I dropped Dori off at Dusty's and told her I'd meet her back there after I had Cal take a look at the hatchback. It had been running rough and loud and I thought he better check it out. Two breakdowns on a deserted highway were enough for one year.

Rolling out from under the car, still on his back, Cal held up a rusted metal part that looked like it had broken in half. He had that long-suffering look on his face that generally meant I was in trouble. "Where in the heck you been drivin', woman?"

"Well, you know, Dori and I went to Mexico."

"Did ya use a *road*?"

"Most of the time."

Sighing deeply, he stood up. "Well, she's sure not reparable."

"What is it?" I stared at the part.

"Muffler."

"I thought it might be." I was proud of myself for correctly identifying the problem, but it didn't last long.

"In all my days I never met anyone harder on a vehicle than you. You oughta take up destruction derby drivin'. Least make some money off it."

"I know. I'm sorry. I'll pay for the repair."

"Bet yer darn tootin' ya will. But it's gonna be a while."

Uh, oh. That sounded way too much like the line he'd used about the motorhome repair. Was he talking days or weeks? "Why's that?"

"Well, I don't just have the part lyin' about."

"You don't?" I glanced at his yard, which was full of nothing but parts. Rusted, mind you, but definitely parts.

"Nope. Gotta send for it. Meantime, I could duct tape it together, or you could just drive her the way she is. They'd know yer comin' before ya got there."

"Couldn't I get a ticket for that?"

"In these parts? Nah."

I considered my options and decided neither duct tape nor deafness worked for me. "I'll just leave it with you 'til it's fixed. I'll be staying here for a while now."

"She got to ya, did she?"

"Huh?"

"Harmony. Them mountains." He nodded his head at the red rocks in the distance. "Our air. Once she gets under yer skin, ya can't let her go. I told ya that the last time you were fixin' ta leave."

"Yes. I guess you did." I looked over at the mountains and back at Cal, whose lack of guile I had come to appreciate. I was reared in the land of little white lies, where no one ever said exactly what they thought. It was supposedly to protect the other person's feelings, but really it was because, above all, *you must be liked.* The plain honesty of the Harmony folks was at first like a foreign language. After being immersed in it for a few weeks, however, I got it and I liked it–the freedom that comes from saying what you mean. Who knew?

"This *is* a beautiful place, Cal." I drew my eyes back to his yard then up at the apartment above his garage and saw his home through *his* eyes. His life *was* beautiful. Simple, and beautiful.

"Yer home too now, woman. Yer home too."

I nodded in agreement.

"Bye, now." He tugged on his cap and walked into the garage with the muffler in tow.

When I walked into Dusty's, I at first thought that Dori must be in the kitchen, because she was nowhere in sight. Then I spotted her at a booth, relaxed back against the seat and smiling. What? I moved around to see who was with her. Malachi. Smiling too. Of course. Not exactly in character for them, but something I had a feeling was rapidly changing.

"Hi." I stood at the end of the booth.

Dori slid over for me to join them.

"I don't want to intrude."

"Just sit down." Dori gave me a *don't be ridiculous* look.

"So what's up?" I sat down, stretched my legs out to the side and crossed my ankles.

"Malachi has offered to drive me and Luke back to Los Angeles."

Wow. Things really were moving fast between those two. "He has?"

"Yeah. He's going to be using L.A. as his base for now."

"Great." I frowned at Malachi. "Then you must think Carrick himself is lurking around down there."

"That'd be speculation on your part. I can't comment."

Oh, so we were back to that, were we? Malachi in secret agent mode? Irritating. "You don't have to. It's not hard to figure out. And you think it's safe for Dori and Luke to move back to L.A.?"

"As safe as anywhere, really. And I'll keep an eye on them."

"I'm sure you will, but you can't be there twenty-four seven."

"They've already made a few arrests in L.A., including the woman at the shelter who was passing information to the cartel," Dori offered as reassurance. "The traffickers try to infiltrate shelters because they don't like to lose their victims to them–it costs them money."

"Great." It didn't make me feel any better. "I don't know." I shook my head. "It sounds too dangerous to me."

"You lived in L.A. your whole life, Syd, and you survived. We'll be fine."

"Yeah, but that was before I became acquainted with people who, you know, sell people and drugs for a living."

"I won't let anything happen to them, Sydney." Malachi's eyes softened as he looked over at Dori.

She looked uncomfortable but pleased as she brushed her long hair away from her face to cover her reaction.

"So where will I be findin' you if I need to?" Malachi shifted his eyes to me. "We'll still be wantin' you to testify when the time comes. For now, though, it'll be fine for you to head back to New York. Carrick is on to much bigger things. Or will ya be headin' back to California too?"

"No. I'm staying here."

"*In Harmony?*" Dori said it so loud that the people at the tables nearby looked over. Then she smiled broadly. "And why would that be?"

"The weather." I smiled back at her. "And the culture. Definitely the culture."

"Sure."

"When are you leaving for L.A.?" I changed the subject.

"Tomorrow."

"So soon?" My heart dropped. I had been with her so much the past few days that it was hard to imagine not having her around.

"Malachi has to get back."

"I understand." I folded my legs under me and put my hand on Dori's arm. "Well then, I guess this is good-bye, for now. I've got to get going. I called Noah for a ride to the ranch and he should be here any time."

"I'll walk you out."

"Malachi." I turned to him before I stood up. "Good to see you again. Maybe at some point we'll be able to meet under normal circumstances."

"It'll be my pleasure, to be sure." His Irish accent was back in full lilt. Amazing how he could turn the thing on and off.

"You take care of yourself and them." I looked pointedly at Dori.

"I will, indeed."

"Good-bye, now."

"Good luck. Good luck. Good luck."

"Good luck. Good luck. Good luck." I said, thinking back to when I heard that good-bye for the first time at Bridie's Pub.

"The Irish farewell again, huh?" Dori looked from one to the other of us.

"Indeed." Malachi tipped his head.

"Well, it's a strange one." Dori scooted out of the booth.

"You'll get used to it." I smiled at Malachi and looked over to where Luke was stacking dishes into the tub at the end of the counter. "Hang on. Let me say good-bye to your brother."

"Sure."

He had lifted the tub and was starting to carry it into the kitchen when I reached him. "Wait a minute, Luke." I stopped him. "You're leaving tomorrow. I want to say good-bye."

"Yes. We are going back to Los Angeles."

"That's great. I hope to see you there sometime."

"Okay." He started to walk off again.

"Wait. Remember when I sent you those postcards from my trip to New York."

"Yes. You sent five."

"That's right. I was wondering if you'd send some to me from your adventures. Maybe one or two from L.A., but I'd also like to have some from that trip you're taking to Alaska someday."

"I can do that. Yes." He nodded.

"Good." I smiled. "I look forward to it. Good-bye, Luke."

"Good-bye." From the distant look in his eye, his mind had already moved on–to Alaska, maybe.

Dori was waiting for me outside the door of the diner. It was cold and she hadn't grabbed her sweater. "You must be freezing." I put my arm around her shoulder.

"It's not so bad. Not nearly as cold as that night in the car in Dry Creek."

"True." I nodded. "I'm really going to miss you."

"I'm going to miss you, too, but L.A.'s not that far. And I'll keep in touch."

"I hope so."

"So, Noah." She smiled at me.

"Yeah." I smiled back.

"Good." She nodded. "Very good."

CHAPTER TWENTY-ONE

Pulling up in front of the diner, Noah left his truck idling on the road, because attached to it was a long trailer. I hurried over and stepped into the passenger seat. "Thanks for picking me up. I'm going to be without a car for a few days." I attached my seatbelt.

"Why is that, again?" Noah glanced over at me from under his cowboy hat as he put the truck in gear.

"The muffler."

"I figured. You could've awakened the dead with the noise it was making. I won't ask how it happened."

"I appreciate that. I already had one talking to by Cal." I pointed my thumb back at the trailer. "I'm sorry I interrupted your work. Whatcha got going on? Are you hauling cattle?"

"No."

"So, what then?"

"You'll see."

"Okay?" Apparently that was the end of the discussion, because Noah moved on to the topics of weather and livestock and hay yields. I felt like I was with V.A. I filled him in on the outcome of Angela's living situation and Dori's move back to L.A.

Noah and I hadn't debriefed our exchange from the night before and the use of the word "love." He wasn't the debriefing type, which was okay with me. Nope. It was a new day. And that morning as we sat in his kitchen over coffee and cold cereal, we were as comfortable with each other as if we'd been together for years.

As Noah parked the truck outside the barn, Mr. Bumbles and Trudy trotted over to us. They too acted like they'd been together for years–an unlikely pair, with Mr. B's lack of ambition and Trudy's strong work ethic. He immediately sat down and started scratching behind his ear, while she was right at Noah's heels as he opened the back of the trailer and lowered the ramp.

I watched as he led one of the most stunning horses I'd ever seen out of the trailer. Its honey-colored coat glistened in the sunlight, offset by its bright white mane and tail. A broad brush of white also ran the full length of its nose. Noah talked softly to it as he walked it over to me. Its ears flickered in response. When he reached me, he handed me the reins.

"Oh." I tentatively held on to them. He knew I had very little experience with horses. "What do you want me to do?" I thought maybe he had to leave right away and wanted me to take it into the barn.

"Her name is Amber Dream."

"Amber Dream, that suits her well." I ran my hand over the broad stripe on her nose, feeling the velvet softness and the warm gentle breeze of her breath as I reached her nostrils.

"And she's yours."

"Mine?" Goosebumps ran from my head to my toes. "What do you mean?"

"I mean, I bought her for you."

"You bought me a horse?"

"I did." He ran his hand over her side.

"I don't understand."

"It's not too difficult. If you're going to be living in Harmony you need a horse."

"You mean you're going to turn me into a ranch hand?"

"No. I mean some of the greatest natural wonders in the world are in Southern Utah, and one of the best ways to get to them is on horseback." His eyes crinkled up at the edges in a smile. "And she'll make a great ranch horse too, if you ever do decide to take up roping and branding."

"Oh yeah, that's gonna happen. You saw how well I did the last time I rode. I could barely stay up on Rosie."

"It'll be different with Amber. She's a Quarter Horse. She's shorter and has powerful hindquarters. And she's very calm."

"There's a real self-esteem booster, hearing you got me a horse with a broad butt to fit my own." I rolled my eyes.

"You have a great butt!" He patted my rump.

"Thanks. I think." I smiled. "But really, Noah. You bought her for *me*?" I still couldn't wrap my head around it as I stared into her huge brown eyes.

"I did. What do you think?"

"I think she's lovely. And if there's such a thing as love at first sight, I think I'm in it." I stroked her back.

"Oh sure, with her and not me?"

"Hm. Let me think about that one. My first sight of you, I thought I had walked into an old Marlboro Man ad, and then you stuck your nose into a book and paid no attention to me, which didn't give love at first sight much of a chance."

"Oh, I was paying attention."

"Sure. I bet I made a great first impression with my chipped tooth and baseball cap."

"I liked it." He grinned. "It was quirky."

220 · SUSAN HART SNYDER

"Quirky. Now there's a word that makes a girl feel all warm and fuzzy." I grinned back.

Noah took the reins from me and draped them over Amber's neck, and then removed his hat, wrapped his arms around my waist and pulled me into him. Kissing my neck, he whispered, "How about this? Does this make you feel all warm and fuzzy?"

"As a matter of fact, it does." I whispered back.

When he raised his head, I kissed him softly on the lips. "Thank you. Amber's the gift of a lifetime. You're a remarkable man." I could feel the tears start to fall from the corner of my eyes. Wiping them away, I reached for the reins. "So where are we going on our first ride?"

"Well, let's see, the sun's still out for a few hours. How 'bout we ride the fence line. It's time I show you the whole place if you're signing on to this outfit." He set his hat back on his head and winked at me from under it. A moment in time I knew right then would stay with me forever.